ABALONE SUMMER

John Dowd

ALASKA NORTHWEST BOOKS™
Anchorage • Seattle • Portland

Library of Congress Cataloging-in-Publication Data
Dowd, John.
    Abalone summer / John Dowd.
        p.   cm.
    Summary: Twelve-year-old Jim, depressed after his father's
death, finds adventure and challenge when he spends the
summer with a Department of Fisheries diver off the rugged
coast of British Columbia's Queen Charlotte Islands.
    ISBN 0-88240-441-5
    [1. Abalone—Fiction.   2. Boats and boating—Fiction.
3. Adventure and adventurers—Fiction.   4. Poaching—Fiction.
5. British Columbia—Fiction.]   I. Title.
PZ7.D7534Ab   1993   93-4250
[Fic]—dc20   CIP
                                                     AC

Edited by Ellen Harkins Wheat
Designed by Alice C. Merrill
Cover illustration by Arthur Shilstone
Map by Vikki Leib

Alaska Northwest Books™
An imprint of Graphic Arts Center Publishing Co.
Editorial office: 2208 NW Market Street, Suite 300
    Seattle, WA 98107
Catalog and order dept.: P.O. Box 10306, Portland, OR 97210
    800-452-3032

Printed in the United States of America

ABALONE SUMMER

CONTENTS

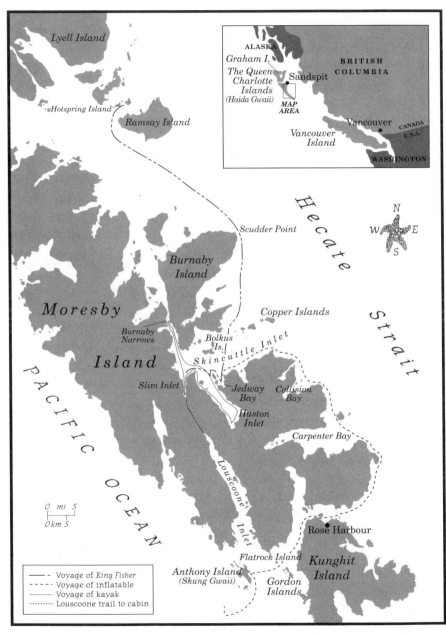

Jim and Julia's Adventures in the Queen Charlotte Islands

one

KITSILANO

Jim Martin tossed the crumpled year-end report card on the table in front of his mother, and swung open the refrigerator door, scanning the shelves critically.

"How come there is never anything worth eating in this dumb thing?" he asked.

There was no response. He poked a finger through the plastic wrap tightly covering a bowl of mashed potatoes.

"Well?" he demanded, reluctant to shift his gaze from the lit interior.

Still no response. He stole a glance over his shoulder. His mother leaned back in her chair, holding Jim's sixth-grade report card at arm's length. Her watery gaze was fixed on some point beyond the wall.

"Jeez," he said. "It's not that bad."

She wiped the corners of her eyes, shook her head, and got to her feet.

"No," she said. "It could have been worse. You could have gotten a D in math too."

"I guess I'm just a dummy."

"Troubled maybe, but no dummy."

Jim reached for a slice of bread and began to spread it thickly with peanut butter.

"I just don't like that school," he snarled. "I hate it! It's run by nerds, and it's boring."

He layered strawberry jam over the peanut butter and took a huge bite, then sauntered to the door of their small apartment and, with a touch of his toe, flicked his skateboard deftly into his free hand.

"I'll be at Marty's," he mumbled.

"Wear your helmet on the ramp and be back by five. We're having a visitor for dinner."

Jim gave no sign that he had heard. He zipped his jacket over his oversize T-shirt and, at the bottom of the steps, dropped the board onto the sidewalk. The afternoon breeze blew warm against his skin. With the ease of a circus pro, he weaved his way past the familiar obstacles on the way to his friend's house.

He was sick of Kitsilano: sick of the tightly packed clapboard houses, the knots of snotty-nosed kids clogging the sidewalk with plastic tricycles, sick of the rows of parked cars and the drunken hobos hanging around the government liquor store. He hated drunks more than anything, hated them from his very core.

Four drunks lounged on the grass in the late afternoon sunlight, passing brown paper bags between them. Jim's eyes narrowed to slits. He pushed the board to gain speed and clattered past close to the feet of one.

"Dirty creeps!" he yelled.

A red-faced, unshaven wino with a blackened, swollen eye rose to his knees and shook a wine bottle after Jim.

There were five boys at the skateboard ramp already. Steven and Roger, both thirteen, stood along the narrow ledge watching Michael, eleven, seesaw back and forth on the curved plywood slopes making a clatter like a train racing over a bridge. Jim's classmate, Marty, was there with his kid brother, Ted. An assortment of bicycles cluttered the long grass beneath a tall spreading chestnut tree, its big green leaves shading a broad expanse.

"Hi, Jim," said Marty.

"Hi! Where's Andy?" asked Jim.

"Grounded. His report card was real bad."

"Mine too. But I guess my mom didn't figure it would do any good to ground me."

He tossed his board onto the ramp and began to work it back and forth, up and down the smooth, rounded slopes alongside Michael. Soon he was feeling relaxed and a little light-headed. It was as close to flying as a kid could get.

The wheels clattered on the ramp joints and rumbled on the boards with a din he loved because it drove the neighbors crazy. He reached the lip of the ramp, turned, and swooped back down the slope, bending his knees and pumping for speed, and then up the other side he soared.

"Helmet!" roared a woman's voice from the house. "You know the rules!"

Marty's mother was leaning out of the kitchen window, shaking an accusing finger. Jim slowed to a low roll, and Marty tossed him a battered hockey helmet.

"Is that so I don't make holes in the ramp with my head?" Jim asked loudly.

But Marty's mother had already retreated. She liked Jim. He had a good heart, but she was worried about him since the car crash that had killed his father. He was the natural leader of the group, but he was angry and took risks, and she didn't want his recklessness to influence the other boys.

Marty swapped places with Michael and swooped back and forth in harmony with his friend.

"You going away this summer?" Marty yelled.

"Nah," Jim said. "Nowhere to go."

"You'll be the only one left around here," said Marty.

"Oh, great!"

"You hear the cops picked up Randy for busting into cars?"

"Yeah. Now there is someone who's really dumb. They say one of the cars belonged to a cop."

"Yeah. They caught Randy inside it."

"He's a jerk."

Other boys arrived and took turns on the ramp. At five minutes past five, Marty's mother flung open the window once again and hollered, "Jim, your mother just called. She wants you to go home right away."

"Rats," said Jim.

He swerved his skateboard off the ramp, catching it before the wheels touched the grass. He tossed the helmet onto the ground and then, with a casual "See ya!" he pushed off, clattering close to the metal fence around the house with the yappy dog. At the corner, he turned so he would not pass the liquor store again, flipped his board off the curb, and swerved down the middle of the side street, weaving between the slalom lines that the city had so obligingly painted.

He wondered who could be coming to dinner. His mother hadn't invited anyone over since the funeral almost two years ago. An angry horn blasted him from behind. He gave a rude one-finger salute, moving over just enough to let the car pass, and ignored the muffled threats coming from the driver.

two
_____

GEORGE

Back home, Jim burst into the kitchen and tossed his board into the closet. The house looked neater than he had seen it in months. He sniffed: spaghetti sauce.

"Jim, put on some clean clothes for supper, please," called his mother from the bathroom.

"You're kidding."

The bathroom door opened. "Please," his mother said softly.

Jim stared in amazement. She was wearing a pretty flowered dress, and her face looked different. "You're wearing makeup!"

"Well, it's a long time since we had someone to supper," she said.

In the hallway he almost collided with Monica, his seven-year-old sister.

"Now I've seen it all: Monica Martin wearing a dress."

"You're just jealous," she quipped.

"Oh, sure. Who's coming tonight, anyway?" Jim asked.

"Mommy's got a boyfriend," she said.

"He is *not* a boyfriend," called a firm voice from the bathroom. "He's an old friend of your father's."

Jim was stunned. Outraged. The thought that his mother might have a boyfriend had never occurred to him. It seemed all wrong. He walked down the hall to his room. There on the bed was a set of clean clothes. Rather than choosing different ones, which he might normally do just to be contrary, he removed his school clothes and put on the clean T-shirt and jeans. Who was this man coming to dinner?

His mind was suddenly filled with the image of his father wrapped around the bent steering wheel of their crumpled station wagon, thick red blood dripping onto his trousers and forming a little puddle on the rubber floor mat. He struggled to push the memory out of his mind but it pressed forward. Squeezing his eyes he tried to drive the picture away, but it wouldn't go. His mind then moved on to the ride in the ambulance, his father strapped to the stretcher next to him, with the medics working frantically over him. Then they had stopped and drawn the blanket up over his father's hastily bandaged head, and Jim had sat there alone, opening and closing his mouth in wordless disbelief.

His sister appeared in the doorway. "Get a load of Mister Cool," she said.

He threw his dirty shirt at her, for once glad of the intrusion.

"Who is this guy Mom's invited?" he asked.

"A fisherman or something," she said.

"A fisherman!"

Jim stared at her to see if she was joking. She wasn't. His mother poked her head into the bedroom doorway.

"That looks better," she said, eyeing him approvingly.

Jim glared at her.

"How do I look?" she asked hesitantly, stepping forward.

"I'm sure *he* will be impressed," said Jim. Then, softening, he added, "You look okay, but sort of . . . younger."

"It's my hair," she said. "I had it cut today. It feels a lot better."

The doorbell rang, and a look of panic crossed his mother's face.

"You kids behave nicely tonight," she pleaded, and headed for the front door, smoothing her dress.

Jim didn't know what to expect, but what he saw surprised him. Fishermen, to him, were fat, red-faced, middle-aged men who sat outside Winnebagos on folding chairs, drinking beer and talking about the salmon they had caught that day. He'd seen them when his family went on their annual camping trip to Texada Island—annual, that is, until two years ago. The visitor was nothing like that. He was tall and lean with dark curly hair and a trimmed black beard. In his hand he carried a bottle of wine, and under his arm a roll of papers.

"Children, this is George McCrae," said their mother brightly.

"So you're Jim and Monica," the man said. "I've heard a few things about you." He held out his hand.

"Don't believe any of it," Jim said, reluctantly shaking the man's hand. It was warm and rough.

"I thought you might like these," George said, and he peeled off a nautical chart before handing two rolled posters to the children. Excitedly Monica spread hers out on the floor: it was of a ballerina in full flight; Jim's was a skateboarder riding his board through space on the rings of Saturn.

"Hey, that's cool," said Jim, warming to the visitor, while Monica stared at her poster, lost in fantasy.

"I hear you're pretty hot stuff on a skateboard," George said.

Jim shrugged awkwardly.

"Supper's ready," came the call from the kitchen.

Steam rose from the large spaghetti bowl in the middle of the table. Alongside it was a brightly colored salad and a plate piled with slices of golden toasted garlic bread.

"George, you can sit there," said Jim's mother, pointing casually to the long-vacant seat at the head of the table.

That was too much for Jim. "No. I'll sit there," he said, his voice slightly shrill. He moved behind the chair.

His mother stared at him. Jim glared back defiantly.

"Sure, I'm easy," George said, softly glancing at Jim's mother. He leaned over and switched his wineglass with Jim's Coke.

Jim sat down. He felt very strange sitting in his father's chair and looking along the length of the table to the flushed face of his mother. She was talking too fast, he thought.

She looked at him and said, "George is a diver."

Jim glanced at his sister. "Monica told me he was a fisherman."

"Well, both, really," said George. "I'm doing contract

research on abalone in the Queen Charlotte Islands, just north of here off the coast."

Jim took a mouthful of spaghetti and deliberately sucked in the tails noisily.

"What's abalone?" he said, taking pains not to display too much interest.

"An abalone is a shellfish like a giant chiton. It has a shell that looks a bit like an ashtray. Come to think of it, the shells are often used as ashtrays," he said. "You may have seen one: the inside of the shell is a beautiful iridescent blue-green. Abalone are excellent eating and very valuable. Divers make lots of money gathering them."

"How much are they worth?" asked Jim, ears pricking up.

"Oh, about sixteen dollars a pound, and a good diver can land three to four hundred pounds a day."

"Wow!" Jim did a quick calculation. "That's more than six grand a day!"

He jumped up from the table and pulled a calculator from a drawer. "That's two million three hundred and four thousand a year," he said. "You must be rich!"

George was laughing.

"No, no," he said, smiling. "I don't actually catch abalone for a living. I study them for the Department of Fisheries. They provide a boat, then pay me to survey the numbers of abalone that are there to help decide whether and when there will be an 'opening.' That's what they call the time when the abalone divers are allowed to catch the quota authorized by the Fisheries Department. Abalone divers only work for a small part of the year and they're only allowed to take a certain amount. When their quota's filled, they go home."

"Still, that's a lot of money for a day's work," said Jim. "I bet a lot of them just pretend to go home."

"That's a problem," admitted George. "And some never even get a license. They just dive and sell the abalone illegally."

"Do you try and catch them?" Jim asked.

"We do sometimes," said George.

"What do you do to them?" asked Jim.

"Oh, Fisheries confiscates their boat and diving gear and sometimes they fine them. But the real bad guys are the illegal buyers; they're a lot harder to catch."

George took an envelope from his jacket and passed a photograph to Jim.

"That's the boat I work from. She's called *King Fisher,* and that's the captain, Andreas Malaspina. He leases the boat to Fisheries when he is not fishing for salmon," he said.

"Looks like a regular fishing boat to me," said Jim, "except for the fancy red rubber dinghy."

"That is no ordinary rubber dinghy," said George. "It's a rigid-hulled, deep-V inflatable and can go over forty miles an hour."

"Wow!"

Handing another photograph to Jim, George said, "This gives you an idea what the country's like."

"I want to see the pictures, please," Monica said impatiently.

Jim handed over the photograph of the boat and then looked at the other; it showed thickly forested hills and calm waters with bright green grass growing in patches along a rocky shore.

"Are those abalone on the rocks?" asked Jim.

"No. Those are mussels and barnacles," said George.

"Does anyone live there?" asked Monica, leaning heavily over the back of her brother's chair.

"No houses for fifty miles," said George.

More pictures followed—of windswept islands covered with seabirds, of huge sea lions straining to watch as killer whales cruised below their rocky perch. There was one of George, dressed in a hooded blue rubber diving suit with bright yellow air bottles on his back and a mask tilted up onto his forehead.

"There's an abalone," he said, pointing to a leathery-looking disk held in his gloved hand. Quickly he shuffled the photographs. "And this is what the shell looks like when the meat has been removed."

"Oh, that's pretty," said Monica. "Like oil on water."

One picture showed a sleek blue fiberglass sea kayak pulled up onto a rocky beach. George said he used it to explore the inlets on his days off.

"It's my escape capsule," he said. "When I've had enough of this world, I climb in and take off."

Jim held the picture in his hand and stared at the graceful boat with its single cockpit. Something about its simplicity appealed to him. With something like that you could be really free.

"Don't hog the pictures," said Monica.

Jim lay in bed staring at the ceiling long after George had left. He thought about the forested hills and protected coves of the Queen Charlotte Islands, of high-speed chases after renegade abalone poachers. But his mind kept returning to the kayak on the beach. Earlier, as the adults had sat sipping coffee in the living room, George had casually asked Jim if he might like to help on the fishing boat that summer.

The suggestion had taken Jim by surprise. He was interested but suspicious. First, he figured it was a way for this guy to butter up to his mother. He was not even sure George was serious. At the time, he had muttered something noncommittal and the conversation had moved on to other topics. As Jim nodded off, he wondered if the offer really had been made.

three
___

A JOB OFFER

The offer was real. The next day, a hand-delivered letter came from the Ministry of the Environment. It read:

> *Dear Jim:*
>
> *It was good to meet you last night. If you are inter-ested in working as my assistant aboard the* King Fisher *this summer, I'd be glad to have you along. The pay is four hundred and fifty dollars a month plus room and board. You can fly up and join me early next week. Let me know ASAP.*
>
> *Regards, George*

"Well, look at this. Your boyfriend has offered me a job this summer," he said, waving the letter at his mother.

"He's not my boyfriend!" she snapped.

"He's offering me four hundred and fifty dollars a month!"

"What?" she said, astonished. "He didn't need to do that!"

Jim looked sharply at his mother.

"Hey. Maybe he thinks I'm worth it," he said.

"I'm not saying you aren't worth it," she said hastily. "It's just that you are only twelve and that's a lot of money."

"I'd get nearly a grand for the summer," Jim quickly calculated.

Jim phoned the number at the bottom of the letter, and a secretary told him to hold. The phone rang again and George came on the line.

"This is Jim. Is that job still available?"

George chuckled. "Sure is," he said.

"I think I'd like to do it," said Jim. "I need the money."

"I have to warn you, though. This isn't an easy job. On a boat you only get time off when there is nothing left to do, and you must always obey the captain."

"Okay."

"And it's often cold and wet in the Queen Charlottes, even in summer."

"Yeah, I figured that."

"Also, there is nowhere to run a skateboard for fifty miles."

"So?"

"So you still want the job?"

"Yeah. It'll beat hanging around here."

"Okay. It's yours. I'll send you a list of what you'll need to bring, along with an airplane ticket for next Monday morning. Any questions?"

"Nope. Well, maybe. Will you show me how to use the sea kayak?"

"Sure," said George. "But first you have to learn to use the inflatable. Driving it will be your work."

At the ramp that afternoon, Jim grabbed a helmet and joined Marty.

"I got a job for the summer," said Jim.

"Doing what?"

"Working on a fishing boat in the Queen Charlotte Islands."

Marty rolled to a halt. "You're what?"

"Figure my mom set it up to get me outta her hair for the summer, which suits me just fine."

Jim turned to where Marty's mother had appeared at the window for her reminder about helmets. He bowed low as he rolled back and forth.

"That's what I like to see," she said, her round face crinkling into a smile. "Of course it would look better if you did up the chin strap!"

"What's the money?" Marty asked Jim.

"Four fifty a month."

"Wow," Marty said. "Some people get all the breaks."

"Yeah, I guess."

That night, Jim dreamed he was in a crowded station. The people were all walking away from him toward a train and he was searching for someone—searching the backs of the heads for a familiar figure. Then he saw him, stepping aboard the train. Jim yelled and tried to run, but his voice didn't work and his feet were too heavy to move. He screamed, but only a hoarse whisper escaped his lips, and the man did not turn around. The door closed, and the train began to move.

"It's okay, Jimmy. It's okay. I'm here."

Jim sat up, wild-eyed. His mother was sitting on the side of his bed.

"Was it the dream again?"

He nodded, sleepily. His mother laid him down and stroked his hair gently until his steady breathing told her sleep had retrieved her son.

Within days, a letter arrived from George with an airline ticket and a list of required clothing. Jim saw George once again when he stopped in on his way to join the *King Fisher*. He came to take Jim's mother out to dinner, while Jim and his sister watched TV late with a babysitter.

George's only comment about the Queen Charlotte trip was, "When you get to Sandspit, you walk out of the terminal and cross the street to the Coast Guard office. Ask for Barry West—if he hasn't already met you." Then he added, "Be sure to bring a few good books. The TV reception is not too great where we're going, specially since we don't have a TV."

four
—

THE QUEEN CHARLOTTE ISLANDS

Jim left for the Queen Charlotte Islands three days later. He was glad he would not be sitting around watching his friends dwindle as they took off on family vacations. He had found an open door and was walking through it, though his stomach was in an uncomfortable knot.

"Feeling a bit nervous?" his mother asked, as she drove him to the airport in their old Datsun.

"Kind of," he admitted. "I guess I still don't trust the cars on the other side of the road."

"I mean about flying into the wilderness."

"Oh, yeah. Sort of."

They parked the car and Jim carried his backpack into the busy terminal building. Half a dozen people stood in line at the Canadian Airlines ticket counter. Two wore workmen's clothing and rugged high boots; another had on a business suit and carried only a briefcase. The other three were women, loaded down with shopping bags and overstuffed suitcases. The women chatted together quietly, but paused when Jim and his mother joined the line.

"Here, give me my ticket," Jim said, tugging it from his mother's hand.

When Jim's turn came, the man behind the counter weighed his backpack, tagged it, and put it in a plastic tub that bobbed along a conveyor belt and disappeared into a hole in the wall. Then, tearing a leaf from the ticket book, he handed Jim a boarding pass. Jim's mother walked with him to the barrier and reached out, saying, "Give me a kiss."

Looking around at the other passengers, Jim gave her a quick peck on the cheek, and then headed for the barrier where a line was forming. Midway, he paused, looked back, and ran and gave her a hug.

"That's better," she said, laughing. "Take care, my little fisherman."

Jim walked quickly back to the gate. He turned and waved to his mother, who summoned an anxious smile.

Jim passed through the security arch, and the buzzer screeched.

"Empty your pockets, please," said the guard.

Into a tray, Jim emptied a pile of coins, a Swiss Army knife, and a slingshot. The guard picked up the slingshot gingerly and waved it at another guard.

"What do you think?" he asked. His companion rubbed his chin thoughtfully.

"Looks like a pretty deadly weapon to me," he said with barely a hint of a smile.

Jim stood by, quietly waiting, as the guard picked up

Jim's knife and opened the blade, touching it lightly with his fingertips. "Holy smokes. This thing's like a razor!" he said. "Where do you think you are going with this?"

"I'm going to work on a fishing boat," said Jim, with a sudden sense of panic that they might take his father's knife away from him.

The guard closed the knife and bounced it in his hand as if making a decision. Then he handed it to Jim. "Keep it in your pocket during the flight, and next time pack it in your luggage. That goes for the slingshot, too," he said sternly.

Relieved, Jim turned to look one more time at his mother and then walked to the waiting room. There were about thirty passengers sitting around in plastic chairs. Beyond the window, he could see a Boeing 727 being serviced by the ground crew. It was probably his plane. Suddenly Jim felt very nervous and very alone. What if nobody was at Sandspit to meet him? What if no one had ever heard of him, or of George? What if he could never get back home?

He jumped as a voice squawked a garbled announcement over a loudspeaker. He had often traveled by plane with his father, and his dad had been able to translate the mechanical voice.

"Is it time to board?" he asked a large woman wearing broad silver bracelets and a heavy silver necklace carved with Indian motifs. The woman nodded.

"You're traveling by yourself?" she asked.

"Yes. It's my first time to the Queen Charlottes."

"Is someone meeting you?" she asked.

"Yes. Mister Barry West," said Jim.

The woman nodded. "Coast Guard," she said knowingly. "He is a good man."

Jim felt better, and joined the group at the gate where the ticket collector was taking their boarding passes and handing back their stubs.

The plane was a large one that still smelled of new carpet and vinyl. The seats were arranged in three rows, four seats together down the middle section and a row of three down each side. Jim's seat was next to a window, and he pressed his face against the thick plastic. On the airstrip, puddles from an overnight shower were drying under the force of the early July sun. Soon they were taxiing forward. The motors roared and the floor pounded beneath him as the plane gathered speed. Jim closed his eyes. What would happen if their plane hit another one at this speed, he wondered. The image of that blanket-covered form beside him in the ambulance flashed through his mind again. He shut it out.

Abruptly the hammering stopped. The plane was free, rising, banking steeply so Jim could look down on the streets of suburban Vancouver, where tiny cars moved in slow motion and tugboats nuzzled log booms on the Fraser River. He searched in vain for their apartment among the neat grid of streets in Kitsalano, and then they were over the harbor and climbing toward the ski area at Cypress.

Patches of cloud flashed past the window.

Before long, the plane had leveled off, and the flight attendant came around with a tray of paper cups filled with orange juice. Jim drank two. Fifteen thousand feet below he glimpsed the hills of Vancouver Island, raw and bare after years of clear-cut logging. He had never seen clear-cut hills before and was shocked at how ugly, how scarred they looked. The Strait of Georgia, between the mainland and Vancouver Island to the west, shimmered in the sun, crisscrossed by the wedge-shaped wakes of dozens of small boats.

Jim took out the airline safety card and glanced over it as the captain explained emergency procedures. The plane was not very full. Across the aisle the business-man sat with four seats to himself, sorting papers in a brown manila envelope.

The next time Jim looked out the window, the sea gleamed a silvery gray with cloud shadows blotched across it. A clump of dark islands began to emerge on the horizon to the north.

"Are those the Queen Charlottes?" he asked the flight attendant as she walked past.

She looked out. "Yes," she said. "They're just coming into view." She handed him a map from the seat pocket and pointed out where they were.

Jim looked with renewed interest out the window at the long fingers of broken mountains protruding far into Hecate Strait, a body of water George had described as one of the nastiest on the coast. Nasty because it was so shallow that fishing boats had been known to hit bottom in the troughs of the waves during bad storms; nasty because for almost a hundred miles, the south shore of Moresby Island, ancient home of the Haida Indians, was virtually uninhabited.

In school they had studied the Haida. He knew they were considered the fiercest of the Pacific Northwest coastal tribes. In the old days, they ranged hundreds of miles from home in huge dugout cedar war canoes to raid the Tlingit to the north and the Makah to the south and bring home slaves.

Looking down, he could imagine them cruising between the islands in their whaling canoes. Somewhere down there he knew lay old village sites with totems and longhouses abandoned after disease had almost wiped out Native populations. What a wonderful place they had chosen for their home, he thought, feeling a twinge of excitement to be leaving the city behind and flying to the land of the Haida.

The flight attendant came around with a club sandwich and a slice of melon, and soon the plane began to slowly drop lower. Below, a small boat peeled back a wedge of waves across a reach of open water. Abruptly the even green trees of the islands gave way to more raw clear-cut slopes, and the pilot announced they were about to land.

The plane swept over the indented coast, which he could now see had clearings with small cabins connected by a twisting dirt road. A thump from somewhere beneath his seat told him the wheels were down. He remembered his panic the first time he heard that thump, and how his father had laughed and explained he should be alarmed only if he didn't hear the wheels lock in place. A pang of desolation gripped his insides. How he wished his father were with him, cracking his bad jokes about seeing the pilot go by on a parachute.

There had been a time when he was angry with his father for dying, for getting in the way of that other car, for abandoning him. Now, skimming above the forests of the Queen Charlotte Islands, he felt only the emptiness of losing his best friend.

The businessman was still reading his stack of

documents as they dropped lower and the treetops reached for the plane's wheels. Just when it seemed as if they'd crash into the waves washing the rocky shore, there was grass, a wind sock on a pole, then a bump, and a roar as the reverse thrusters kicked in and the plane surged to slow down on the runway. Ponderously, it turned and taxied toward a cluster of small tan buildings dominated by a control tower and surrounded by a variety of small planes and helicopters. The businessman put his papers away in his briefcase.

As Jim stepped off the plane and made his way down wobbly aluminum steps, a chill breeze tugged his jacket. Ragged fluffy clouds marched down from the north carrying occasional drops of rain that dried as soon as they splotched the tarmac. He followed the rest of the passengers to the terminal buildings and, once inside, looked anxiously around the crowd in the waiting room. A man in a dark blue uniform stepped forward.

"Are you Jim Martin?" he asked.

Jim noticed the Coast Guard insignia on his shirt. His short curly dark hair looked like it had been groomed smooth by the wind.

"That's me," he said. "You must be Mister West."

The man smiled and shook Jim's hand warmly.

"Barry's my name," he said. "Your timing is great: not too late for lunch and there's a chopper going down island this afternoon."

"You mean I get to ride in a helicopter?" said Jim incredulously.

"Yep. There is one doing a drop-off to the Fisheries protection boat at Rose Harbour, and George arranged for you to fly down with it."

A crowd had formed around the luggage area and

the three women passengers struggled by with their bags.

"Have a nice holiday," said the lady with the silver jewelry. Jim's pack appeared on the conveyor belt, and he was trying to pick it up when a tall, burly man pushed him aside roughly and grabbed a big cardboard box tied with rope. HOLD FOR *DARK SABLE* was written in bold letters across its top.

"Hey!" Jim protested.

The man turned and glared right through him. Jim gulped and dropped his gaze. Around the man's thick neck was a tattooed ring of lines like a close-fitting necklace, and below were the words CUT ALONG THE DOTTED LINE. On his forearm was another tattoo, this one of a diver's helmet. The letters H-A-T-E were spaced across the knuckles of his right hand, L-O-V-E across his left. He wore a faded red plaid shirt and torn jeans, and his running shoes were so tattered his toes showed through. Jim stood back as the man swung by with what was obviously a heavy box, then he slung his own pack on his back and walked out into the sunshine with Barry.

In the parking lot, they passed the tattooed man again, putting his box in the back of a battered pickup truck. He cast a sharp glance at Barry as he climbed into the cab.

"Did you see the tattoo on that guy's neck?" Jim whispered.

"Yeah. He's new around here."

"He's a diver," said Jim.

"One of the poachers," said Barry.

"Why don't you arrest him then?"

"Gotta catch him with illegal abalone first," said Barry. "Are you hungry?"

"Always," said Jim, with a grin.

Barry took Jim across the street to the Coast Guard station and introduced him to Corporal Raymond, the duty officer, and then led him to the refrigerator and the familiar supplies of peanut butter, strawberry jam, and white bread, and invited him to help himself. Jim scooped the peanut butter from the jar, plastered it on the soft bread, coated it with jam, then wolfed it down.

"Boy, you *are* hungry," observed Barry.

five

CHOPPER
TO SOUTH MORESBY

After a short guided tour of the Coast Guard station, there was still time for Jim to do some exploring of his own. He headed back across the street. His plane had continued to Prince Rupert, and the clutter of cars related to its arrival and departure had dispersed. A flock of gulls repossessed the runway, and an enterprising raven, busy emptying the garbage can by the terminal door, was the only other creature in sight. Jim walked along the perimeter fence, past a couple of deserted helicopter maintenance hangars. He wondered which of the machines he would fly in. What would Marty and the others think when he told them he had flown in a helicopter?

Sandspit Airport was built on the end of a low wooded peninsula that reached down from the forested mountains of Moresby Island and out into Hecate Strait. A narrow blacktop road edged the airfield, then ran past a brown wooden hotel to Skidegate Inlet, where it turned sharply west and followed the shoreline next to the sprawling logging town of Sandspit.

At the turn of the road, a pier extended into the sea. Jim walked onto the sturdy rough planks with gaps that left him dizzy, and sniffed the sea air loaded with the smells of creosoted logs and dried fish. The battered pickup truck he had seen at the airport was parked on the end of the pier, and men were unloading provisions onto a pallet poised to be swung over the side with a crane.

Some Haida boys about his own age were fishing for small silvery fish that wriggled frantically as they were hauled up. They pulled the tiny fish up from between the mussel-encrusted pilings in a detached, almost automatic way, popping them in a bucket to be kept alive and used as bait for bigger fish.

Jim walked to the edge of the pier and looked down. He was surprised how far it was to the boat below. He knew about low tides, but this one looked like the bottom had dropped out of the ocean. In the boat, two deckhands worked above an open hatch, grabbing onto the loaded pallet and lowering it to a third man in the hold. The boat appeared to be made almost entirely of aluminum, with a small sturdy wheelhouse that tilted forward. On top of the wheelhouse sprouted a nest of radar scanners and radio aerials. A green tarp had been thrown back from some deck cargo and Jim could see rows of dark green scuba tanks.

A man, whose tattoos and battered shoes Jim instantly recognized, strode out of the wheelhouse. He glanced up at Jim, then cursed and turned quickly to the deck cargo.

"Cover that up!" he bellowed to the deckhands.

Jim backed away hastily. For a few minutes he watched the Haida boys fish, then gingerly edged up to the corner of the pier and looked back down at the fishing boat, which the crew had now finished loading and were preparing for sea. Across her stern, in letters almost obscured by exhaust grime, were the words DARK SABLE. Jim turned and jogged back to the Coast Guard office.

"The man with the tattoos is just leaving in a boat called *Dark Sable,*" he said. "They have lots of scuba tanks on deck."

"Good," said Barry.

"Good?"

Barry smiled faintly. "Do you want anything from the store?" he asked. "This may be your last chance for a while."

"But he's getting away!" said Jim.

"He's allowed to carry scuba tanks on his boat," said Barry. "The trick is to catch him with the scuba tanks *and* the illegal abalone. Let's go to the store."

Barry and Jim got into one of the Coast Guard pickups and drove the mile along the coast road to the general store. It was a well-stocked grocery store with a large hardware department and a whole wall of fishing lures and spools of nylon. Jim had taken thirty dollars from his bank account in Vancouver and now spent most of this on such essentials as gum, Hershey bars, and Reese's Pieces.

Barry peered into Jim's plastic bag and grinned. "Yep," he said, "I'd say you have everything you need there."

The helicopter was a Hughes 500: a glass bubble just

right for two people and their luggage, with a brightly painted orange motor, and long, limp rotor blades that gave it a wilted look as it sat like a dead dragonfly on the tarmac. Barry introduced Jim to the pilot, Tex, who was standing just inside the hangar office.

"Do they call you Tex because you're from Texas?" asked Jim.

"Ah guess," drawled Tex, with a toothy smile.

Jim liked him. He was not a big man, not as big as Texans were supposed to be, and he wore sneakers instead of cowboy boots. Jim felt immediately comfortable around him. Tex was dressed in a brown flight suit with zippered pockets and slots for pencils on his trouser leg. His open nylon bomber jacket said QUEEN CHARLOTTE ISLANDS AIR SERVICE on the front. His bright blue eyes watched Jim steadily from behind rimless glasses.

"Reckon you'd like one of these flight suits," he said.

"Looks pretty cool," admitted Jim.

"You'll have to grow some first," said Tex.

Tex put Jim's pack onto a handcart loaded with boxes of provisions and some canvas mailbags closed with padlocks. He filed the day's flight plan over the telephone while an assistant hauled the cart out to the helicopter and stowed the freight. Jim was to be the only passenger. Tex helped him up into the copilot seat—a tall bucket seat with a full-harness safety belt that buckled at his navel.

"Say hello to George, Andreas, and Julia for me," Barry said. "Tell George I'll be down to Rose Harbour in a week."

"Who's Julia?" asked Jim suspiciously.

"That's Andreas's daughter," said Barry. "She's about your age, I'd say."

"You're kidding," said Jim in dismay. "George never told me there was a girl there!"

"He may not have known," said Barry. "She works summers on the *King Fisher*. Only went down last week. Don't worry. She's nice. You'll like her."

Jim was furious. He suddenly felt trapped, and was on the point of jumping out of the helicopter and taking the next plane home when Barry closed the flimsy oval door and backed away just before Tex flipped switches. With a whine, the rotors began to turn. Faster and faster they spun until the motor caught and its power surged through the machine.

Through an aging military surplus helmet fitted with a microphone headset, Tex spoke to the air traffic control tower. His eyes flicked across a panel of dials, his hands gripping a movable control column similar to ones Jim had seen in video arcades. The roar of the engine increased, and Jim's heart pounded in his throat. Some invisible hand was letting go, and the helicopter rose to the height of the hangar, leaving Jim's stomach down somewhere beneath his seat. The bubble tilted forward and Jim gulped as he looked straight down onto the perimeter fence. Then, like a piece of dandelion fluff, it lifted up and zoomed over the Coast Guard buildings, white painted houses, and tall trees, until Sandspit was reduced to bright spots where dark green forest met pale green water.

The helicopter followed the coastline. Waves broke along the rocky shore, and beds of brown kelp floated in the shallows. The weather looked like it was improving, and sun glowed on the treetops and baked the mossy clearings. A trail of waves led across the water to a gray aluminum fishing boat running against the stiff northerly breeze. Jim watched spray envelop the craft. It was the *Dark Sable*, heading south in the same direction as they were.

Moments later they were over open water and approaching a steep island that bore the scars of heavy logging.

"There's Skedans," yelled Tex above the roar of the motor, as he pointed to a site on shore to the right.

Jim stared down at a cove protected by rocks. He could make out some old buildings in a clearing and thin colorful boats on the beach.

"Only a Haida watchman lives there now," said Tex. "It used to be a major Native village."

Jim searched the area for signs of life.

"Are those Haida canoes on the beach?" he asked.

Tex maneuvered the helicopter so he could see better.

"No, those are kayaks," he said. "South Moresby is crawlin' with kayakers lately. These days, the Haida use aluminum fish boats."

Jim was about to ask what had happened to the village but it was so noisy he decided to leave further questions for later. Beneath the chopper, islands with ragged rocky shorelines grew out of the sea. To his right Jim glimpsed long, narrow stretches of water that seemed to penetrate the very heart of the mountains on South Moresby Island.

Tex leaned toward Jim, cupped his hand around his mouth, and nodded to a steep landmass dead ahead.

"That's Lyell Island, where environmentalists and the Haida blockaded the roads to stop the logging a few years ago. They even had the tribe elders out there. It was quite an event."

Jim stared at the scarred hillside and broken trees lying crisscrossed over the land.

"Didn't the loggers take the trees after they cut them?"

"They took only the very best."

Beyond Lyell Island, a cluster of forested rocky islands came into view. Near the middle of the group, anchored in a protected cove, a fishing boat gleamed white in the afternoon sun.

"That's Hotspring Island," yelled Tex, "and there's the *King Fisher.*"

six

THE *KING FISHER*

The boat looked strangely toylike, with a large hatch toward the back and tall poles bristling from the main cabin and wheelhouse. As they lost altitude, Jim saw three people come on deck. One, whom he recognized as George, climbed into a red inflatable with twin motors and headed for a gravel spit that reached from Hotspring Island to another island next to it.

Tex positioned the helicopter over the gravel spit and set it down softly on the barnacle-encrusted stones. "Wait here!" he yelled, taking off his helmet.

Jim sat in his harness while Tex scrambled out and around the front of the helicopter to Jim's door. He unbuckled Jim's harness, then led him, bent double, to a spot clear of the spinning rotors.

He pointed to the ground. "Wait!" he yelled, then hurried back to collect Jim's pack and a bundle of mail.

By this time George had beached the inflatable and was striding toward Jim.

"Welcome to the Queen Charlottes!" he shouted above the noise, shaking Jim's hand. George took the mail from Tex and slapped him jovially on the shoulder. The two men stood yelling into each other's ears for a minute, then Tex turned, ducked under the rotors, and scrambled back into the helicopter. With a roar and a scattering of sand and seaweed, the machine lifted off the beach and sped away over the tops of the trees on Hotspring Island, leaving Jim's ears ringing in the silence.

"He used to fly those during the Vietnam war," said George, as they loaded the mailbag and Jim's pack aboard the inflatable. "They gave him a chestful of Purple Hearts."

Jim knew about Purple Hearts. At least he knew that usually you had to get wounded or die to get one. He climbed into the inflatable, and George pushed off from the shore, stepped in, and started the engines.

"How come you never told me there'd be a girl on the boat?" Jim blurted out, as they crunched across the barnacle-covered rocks and weaved their way around patches of kelp that looked like wet brown lasagna noodles.

"I didn't know," said George. "But don't worry. She's ten and plenty tough—a real nice kid."

Jim snorted. His friends at home would laugh themselves sick when they heard he had spent his whole summer trapped on a boat with a ten-year-old girl.

They pulled alongside the *King Fisher*.

"Pass me that line, young fella," called a man dressed in rough woolen clothing and knit hat pulled low over a weathered, furrowed brow. Wrinkles crowded the corners of his pale blue eyes.

Jim passed him the bow line. George scooped up Jim's backpack and passed it up to a skinny, freckled girl who leaned over the rail. She had a short honey blond ponytail and the same light blue eyes. She cast a quizzical glance at Jim, then hauled the heavy pack aboard as if it were empty. Jim and George scrambled over the rail and stood on the deck.

"I'm Andreas," the man said, shaking Jim's hand warmly. "And this is my daughter, Julia."

Jim shook hands with Andreas and nodded noncommittally to Julia, who stood back watching him with curiosity.

"Julia, show Jim where he'll be living," Andreas said.

Jim slung his pack across his shoulder and reluctantly followed Julia inside the wheelhouse. It was warm and the air smelled of engine oil, stew cooking, and damp clothing. A large spiked wooden wheel commanded a view of the foredeck and beyond. Jim peered at a glass dome mounted on the dash.

"This is the wheelhouse, where we steer the boat, and that's the compass," said Julia. She pointed to the different instruments. "And this is the radar and that's the sonar which is like underwater radar. It shows where the fish are. And that over there is the marine radio for talking to other boats."

She stood at the top of a short flight of stairs leading forward to other rooms, and looked back, waiting for Jim. "Have you ever been on a fishing boat before?"

Jim was on the verge of inventing an elaborate story about his experience on other boats. Instead he simply said, "No," with a sigh.

"Then I'll just have to show you everything, won't I?"

She led the way down the narrow wooden steps to a cozy cabin lined with dark wood. It was brightened by two portholes on each side. Books were nestled into neat wooden shelves.

"This is the galley, where we cook our meals," Julia said.

A table to Jim's left had a ledge around it to stop plates falling off when the boat rocked, Julia explained. On his right, a pot, which was the source of the delicious cooking aromas, simmered on a gimballed stove—it was hinged to move with the rocking of the boat.

"That's an oil stove," said Julia. "It has those rails to stop the pots from sliding off in rough seas." Jim turned on the tap over a small stainless steel sink beside the stove.

"First thing you'd better learn around here," said Julia, "is that you never waste water or Dad goes bananas."

A narrow passage led forward.

"That's the head," she said. Then seeing Jim's uncomprehending face, she added, "You know—the can, the toilet."

"Oh," said Jim. It looked miserably cramped, with a tiny porcelain toilet surrounded by handles and levers.

"The instructions are on the wall," she said, "and you'd better get them right or the thing floods and makes a yucky mess."

Jim despaired; even the toilets were threatening.

The last thing he wanted to do was to screw up, make a mess on the floor, and have to call Julia for help. He was beginning to think home looked pretty attractive.

"This is your bunk," continued Julia.

Jim's jaw dropped. "Looks about right for a dwarf," he said.

"No, silly, your feet go in there, and it goes way back. It's a storm bunk. That way you don't fall out in rough weather!"

Jim peered into a hole that extended into the bulkhead. To his relief, the mattress continued inside, but he didn't like being called silly.

Beside his bunk was a porthole almost as big as his head. Condensation had formed on the brass rim.

"It's your job to see that this porthole is closed when we are under way," said Julia. "Otherwise your bed gets wet."

Jim looked forlornly out at the green wavelets and the rocky shore of the nearby island. Beyond, sun splashed yellow light on the tips of the trees. He tossed his pack into the corner and flopped down on his bunk, smacking his head hard on a shelf he had not noticed.

"Watch your head around here," said Julia. "On boats there are lots of things to hit your head on or trip you up."

"So I see," he muttered, holding his head, wishing he had never left Vancouver.

"Cheer up," Julia said kindly. "You get used to it."

She turned around in the narrow passage. "This is George's bunk," she added. "I usually sleep in the galley and Dad sleeps in the wheelhouse. He likes to know what's going on even when he's asleep."

Jim extricated himself from his tunnel bunk and

followed Julia back into the galley, where George and Andreas sat at the table, holding thick mugs of coffee.

"Well, what do you think?" said George.

"Different," said Jim.

Andreas laughed.

"Are you kids ready for some supper?" he asked.

"Soon," said Julia. "I'll just show him around on deck."

Jim looked appealingly at George, but the two men were already lost in conversation. Frowning, he followed Julia through the wheelhouse and out on deck.

"On a boat we call the left side 'port' and the right side 'starboard,' " she said. Jim flinched.

"No kidding," he snapped, staring across the water at something flashing.

"Hey!" Julia shot back. "I didn't ask you to come. We're stuck with each other so we might as well be friends."

Jim looked at her in surprise. "I guess," he said. "Look. What's that?"

"Kayakers," said Julia. "They come to soak in the hot pools on the island. It's great for kayaking here. I have my own kayak."

Jim stared in amazement.

"You do? Here?"

"Sure. Come see," she said, relieved to have found something to interest this difficult person.

She led the way past the wheelhouse to the cramped foredeck, where the upside-down shapes of two kayaks occupied most of the available space.

"This one's mine," she said, turning it over with ease. "I bought it with my own money."

"Wow!" said Jim, genuinely impressed. "It's cool."

The kayak had a red deck with black oval hatches fore and aft. Black bungee cord crisscrossed the deck, and a small white rope tucked into a groove on deck led to what Jim figured was a rudder.

"And that one's George's?" asked Jim, pointing to a blue kayak.

"Yeah. Sometimes he takes off for a week at a time," she said.

Continuing her tour of the boat, Julia showed Jim how the anchor winch worked, where the scuba tanks were kept, and how the compressor for refilling them with air was operated. Then she led him onto the wheelhouse roof.

"My dad gets real mad if he catches you up the mast," she said. "That means, don't let him catch you." And she swung up onto the metal steps that stuck out of the mast and climbed like a monkey to the radar scanner.

"Down!" roared a voice from below. "You know you're not allowed up there."

Andreas stood on deck glaring up at his daughter.

"I was just showing Jim where things are," she pleaded, as she quickly retreated.

"Yeah, sure. Now come in and eat."

Big bowls of rich brown stew steamed on the galley table. They all sat down, and Jim realized how hungry he was once again. He tasted the thick stew.

"You like it?" asked George.

"Yeah, it's good," said Jim, helping himself to a piece of bread which he dipped in the stew.

"It's venison. Andreas shot a deer on the island last week."

Jim paused and examined a piece of the meat. He shrugged. "Tastes great."

Jim felt better after the meal. Julia washed the dishes while he dried and stacked them in special slotted shelves. He was surprised to see it was almost ten o'clock and yet it was still light outside. Wearily he rolled his sleeping bag down the narrow tunnel of the storm bunk, removed his jeans and T-shirt, and climbed into bed, hardly able to believe that only that morning he had been in Vancouver.

seven

HOTSPRING ISLAND

When Jim awoke, he stared at the low ceiling for a moment before he remembered where he was. Someone somewhere above him was hammering, and the sound seemed to pierce his head. He crawled out of his bunk and pulled on his clothes. George's sleeping bag was open and empty. Peering out the porthole, he was surprised to see the sun shining gold like honey on the kelp-covered rocks. He padded barefoot into the galley, where Julia sat cross-legged, munching cereal. She was wearing a T-shirt and red shorts. A stubby pencil in her hand was poised above a crossword puzzle.

"What's a six-letter word beginning with P? The clue is 'hot stuff spotty.' "

Jim blinked.

"Morning. How'd you sleep?" asked Andreas.

"Fine," said Jim groggily. Then, "What's the banging?"

"George is building a box for the compressor," said Andreas.

"We're staying here for the day," Julia announced happily. "Daddy says we can go ashore and explore."

Jim sat at the table.

"Pepper," he said.

"Pepper?" said Julia, puzzled. Jim had nothing to put pepper on.

"Hot stuff spotty."

"Oh! Of course. Good. Hey, you're quick."

"Tell my teachers that."

After breakfast, Julia rowed Jim ashore in the skiff, expertly maneuvering it through a maze of kelp and submerged rocks. Together they dragged the light aluminum boat up the pebble beach to a barrier of storm-beached logs. Jim was relieved to be away from the incessant throb of the generator and the smell of diesel fumes. The beach had the fresh smell of wet sand and decaying seaweed.

A cacophony of screeching greeted their arrival as a gang of ravens hopped about on the limbs of an old snag.

"I hate ravens," said Julia in disgust. "Hell's Angels, Daddy calls them." She tossed a rock ineffectually in their direction. "They always stay just out of range," she muttered.

Jim picked up a round pebble, carefully fitted it to his slingshot, and let fly. There was a sharp crack as the stone shattered a dead branch in the midst of the mob. With a croak of surprise, the ravens rose together and flapped to the far end of the beach, where they set up an even greater clamor.

"Hey, that's pretty cool," said Julia. "Show me how you do that."

Jim showed her how to select the right stone, draw, and release it cleanly. It was a relief to find something Julia was not an expert at. For half an hour they hung around in the sunshine. Julia practiced with the slingshot while Jim refined her technique and skipped flat stones across the bay.

"If you promise not to tell, I'll show you the secret watchtower," said Julia.

"It won't be secret if you show me," Jim pointed out.

She looked at him sharply. "Will you keep the secret?"

"Sure," Jim nodded.

"Cross your heart."

Jim pulled an exasperated face, and crossed his heart.

Julia leapt from log to log, laughing, and then plunged down a path that was barely noticeable. Jim followed, pushing through stiff, noisy salal bushes and waist-high ferns loaded with bright green new fronds reaching for the light that filtered through the canopy. Then he was running noiselessly over a soft path blanketed with hemlock and spruce needles, while about him the forest opened up with tall trees standing like pillars on the gently rising ground. They stopped and stared up until Jim felt dizzy.

"It's like being in church, don't you think?" said Julia.

"It sure beats any church I've seen."

Julia dived off the trail and led Jim up a gentle hill. They pushed through a grove of young cedars and clambered over a huge fallen tree covered with a miniature forest of delicate ferns and brilliant green moss. Jim stopped for a moment, staring at a colony of bright orange mushrooms that grew like a display of tiny parasols from the shady side of the fallen trunk.

"Come on," Julia called impatiently. She was standing in front of an old dead tree over ten feet wide at the base. A long-forgotten windstorm had snapped off its top fifty feet from the ground.

"Well, here it is," she said.

Jim looked around.

"Here is what?" he asked.

"The watchtower," she said, going down on her knees and crawling into a low cave beneath the roots of the huge tree.

Jim followed. The dark earth smelled of mushrooms and dampness. Inside, the ancient tree was entirely hollow and heavy with the fragrance of decay. Blue sky winked through a ragged hole at the top. As Jim's eyes adjusted to the gloom, he noticed that a series of steps protruded from the walls, formed by the knots of old branches more resistant to rot than the heartwood. It looked like a long way up, but Julia was already climbing quickly, at times using the steps, at others pressing her back against the wall while walking her feet up on the other side.

"Are you coming?" Julia's voice sounded muffled and distant.

Jim gulped and followed, feeling the steps with his hands and feet. Halfway up he paused and rested, his back jammed against the wall, legs shaking from the effort.

"Don't stop or you get tired," Julia called.

He looked up to where she sat on a platform at the top looking down at him. None of the kids he knew would even think of making a climb like this. He reached for the next hand grip and moved on.

Puffing and covered with cedar dust, Jim gratefully crawled beside Julia onto the ledge made out of old planks.

"You're the only other person I know who's climbed it," she said, smiling at him proudly. "Even my older cousin chickened out, and he's a teenager."

Jim looked around and whistled.

"Wow!" he said. "What a view!"

To the east and north he could see dozens of little islands. Below, swinging at anchor in the bay, *King Fisher* gleamed in the sunshine, caressed by long feathery tendrils of seaweed that reached out from the green depths.

"Did you build the platform?" Jim asked.

"Oh no," she said. "This was here."

"Who built it?"

Julia shrugged. "Pirates maybe, or the Haida."

"I'll bet it was the Haida. They could see war parties coming for miles from up here."

"They probably hid the women and children here when there was a raid," said Julia.

"And threw their spears down on their enemies," said Jim, peering carefully over the edge.

With their legs swinging over the edge of the platform, they ate a lunch of cheese on rolls. It was fun to be able to see so much from their perch but feel that they were invisible. When they saw the inflatable leave *King Fisher* with Andreas and George and come toward the shore, they hurried down and set up an ambush in the tall trees. When they heard George and Andreas coming, with a screech Julia fell upon the intruders and Jim leapt out at them. Andreas and George raised their arms in surrender.

"We'll take 'em as slaves," announced Julia. "This one with the funny hat will be our cook. The one with the black furry face can go collect abalone for supper."

"We've brought your swimsuits," said the slave with the furry face. Julia grabbed their suits and took off at full speed with Jim close behind. Down the hill they ran, through some dark second growth, then out into the open, close to a small abandoned cabin. Not far beyond it, nestled beneath a rock overhang, lay a natural hot-spring pool big enough for a dozen people at a pinch, but just perfect for four. Steam rose from the pool and from a small stream that fed it. Natural shelves in the rock wall dripped with wax from countless candles.

Between the hot pool and a gravel beach stood a simple slat-sided shed covering another hot pool.

"You can change in those bushes," Julia said, pointing. "I'm going to use the shed."

Quickly Julia and Jim changed into their swimsuits. The water was so hot it took several minutes for Jim to ease into it fully. But then he laid back and stared at the mares' tails creeping across the sky from the west. Andreas and George joined them in the pool.

"Those clouds mean we'll see a change in the weather soon," predicted Andreas.

They lounged in the pool until they grew hungry. Then, almost too relaxed to walk, they stumbled back to the beach and motored out to *King Fisher,* towing the skiff. Jim almost fell asleep over his supper, and crawled into his sleeping bag long before the sun had set.

eight

SOUTH TO SKINCUTTLE

Jim emerged reluctantly from the grip of a dream in which his sister was riding a skateboard through flooded fields while he stumbled after her on foot as the ground shook. Suddenly he was wide awake. The bed lurched and vibrated. He sat up, banged his head, then slumped back on his elbows and groaned. A pounding came from the direction of the bow and a steady throb filled the cabin. Jim drew himself to the porthole and looked outside. He was glad he had closed it securely last night because outside, gray waves speckled with raindrops sped by. In the distance, gray land merged wetly with gray sky. Occasional rushes of water dashed against the thick glass as the bow buffeted the waves.

Jim checked his watch. It was six thirty. He dressed and shuffled unsteadily into the galley. It was empty. In the wheelhouse he found Andreas, George, and Julia crowded around the radio and staring forward into the distance. Andreas was at the wheel.

"Fisheries has stopped your friend in the *Dark Sable,*" Julia said to Jim.

George put binoculars to his eyes and studied the horizon through the slapping windshield wipers. A voice crackled on the radio.

"Tango Charlie, this is Romeo Zulu. Looks like they got rid of the goods. They're clean."

"Damn!" said George.

"Who was that?" asked Jim.

"Fisheries talking to the Coast Guard," said George.

"They dumped the abs when they saw the cutter," Andreas surmised.

"What a waste," said Jim.

"Chances are they won't waste them," said George. "The poachers will have put them in bags and will just go back later to get them."

"Let's find the bags and let the abs go," said Jim.

George smiled. "That would make looking for a needle in a haystack easy," he said.

The *King Fisher* plunged and reared as they left the protection of Ramsay Island and headed into the southeast wind. Ahead, Burnaby Island faded to shadow as rain swept its slopes.

George emerged from the galley. "Drink this," he said, shoving a mug of hot chocolate into Jim's hands.

Jim gripped the counter and sipped the sweet hot drink. He watched in awe as gray walls of water rushed toward them. Just when it seemed certain the bow would plunge beneath a huge wave, the perky little boat lifted miraculously up the wall and hung, poised, before plunging down the other side.

"You like this?" Andreas asked.

Jim nodded unconvincingly. "It's like skateboarding."

"Wait till we get around Scudder Point," Andreas said. "It'll be really lumpy there."

Just what I need, thought Jim grimly.

It took over two hours to reach Scudder Point. Surf crashed against the fringe of black rocks, exploding as high as the treetops. A white light winked forlornly from a tower on the headland. As Andreas predicted, the sea got worse. *King Fisher* rolled and plunged as she ran for the protection of the Copper Islands and Skincuttle Inlet. Jim regretted the mug of hot chocolate. His limbs had gone limp and his stomach hovered somewhere in his throat.

"Put your head out the door and get some fresh air. You'll feel better," yelled Andreas. "But hold tight. You don't want to go overboard in this weather."

Jim gripped the door frame and thrust his face into the wind. Raindrops stung his skin and drove icy needles through his clothes, but he began to feel less like dying.

Mercifully, the seas dropped as *King Fisher* passed inside the Copper Islands, and soon the waves were reduced to shivers that chased one another across the flat waters of Jedway Bay. George and Andreas made the boat fast to a buoy, and Julia emerged unsteadily from the galley, looking very pale.

"Were you seasick too?" she asked.

"Almost," he said.

As if to comfort them, a patch of sunshine moved across the forested hills above them. It played lightly with the colors of the bay, and bathed them briefly in its warmth before moving on.

nine

THE MAKING
OF A BOATMAN

For the next three weeks, the *King Fisher* remained on the buoy in Jedway Bay. They were surrounded on three sides by steep hills covered with old-growth forest, while to the north lay the protected waters of Skincuttle Inlet and the Bolkus and Copper islands. Less than a century before, the bay had been the site of a flourishing Haida village; later it supported a small mining town. Now the forest had claimed back the land.

After their rough introduction, weather conditions improved. Sunshine baked *King Fisher,* and Julia spread all the cushions and mattresses out on deck to get rid of the musty dampness. It was warm enough for T-shirts, shorts, and bare feet.

Each day George and Jim took the inflatable to survey the abalone beds. The first morning, George showed Jim how to check the oil, connect the fuel lines, and start the two twenty-horsepower motors. George was a patient teacher, and Jim, for the first time he could remember, found himself an eager student. When time came for the first lesson in boat handling, George went over the safety check procedure: no loose lines in the water, no gas spilled in the bottom of the boat, fuel primed, nothing loose that might bounce about and cause damage, then start the engines. He covered Jim's hand with his on the controls and eased the throttle forward. The propellers engaged with a bump, edging the boat through a veil of engine smoke that hung above the glassy sea. With steady pressure, he pushed on Jim's hand, and the little boat surged forward, engines snarling. It felt to Jim as if the power came straight from George's hands.

At less than half throttle, the boat skimmed along over the surface of the water, and George said they were "planing." Jim turned the wheel from one side to the other, and the boat turned like a skateboard. He looked back at the S he'd made with the wake and laughed. George looked pleased. He liked Jim's eagerness and the way he learned so quickly.

"Is that the fastest she'll go?" Jim yelled.

By way of answer, George pressed forward on the throttle. The motors screamed. Jim was jammed back into his seat as the bow lowered to horizontal and they shot across the bay. Wind rushed through his hair and wind tears began streaming from his eyes. George eased the throttle back.

"It's bad for the motors to go that fast for long," he said.

"This thing is wild," said Jim enthusiastically.

George's job was to map the abalone population of

South Moresby so the appropriate number of permits could be issued for commercial fishing. To do this, he would dive, mark out a ten-yard-square area on the bottom, then count and measure all the abalone inside the square. He would also count other inhabitants such as starfish, sea urchins, and kelp. Just for Skincuttle Inlet, he had fifty sites marked on his chart.

Jim's job was to keep watch in the inflatable, pass George things he needed, and stand by on the VHF radio. In an emergency, he was to recall George by banging a steel bar with a hammer underwater. If George surfaced far away and held his arm in the air, Jim's instructions were to start the motor, pull the anchor (never pull up the anchor before the engine is running, George insisted), and go pick him up. But before Jim could be entrusted with that job, George made him practice by repeatedly approaching a piece of floating driftwood.

"You'd have drowned me," he cried, as Jim ran the flotsam down on the first try. "Always approach from downwind if the person is swimming free, and from down current if the person is holding onto a buoy or rock."

Jim tried again and again.

"That's more like it. You throttled back a little too soon that time. And remember to hit neutral fast or you could cut my legs off with the propeller. Try again."

Then, at last, "That's it. That's very good, Jim."

The first time George dived, Jim watched with growing concern as he pulled on a thick blue neoprene dry suit that covered every piece of exposed skin except for an oval that included his eyes, nose, and mouth, puckered together by a tight-fitting hood. Even his beard was inside. Huge black fins were attached to his neoprene booties. George strapped one of the scuba tanks into a frame, slung it onto his back, and sat on the side of the boat.

"Pass me the weight belt," he said.

Jim grabbed the belt and pulled, but it didn't budge. It took both his hands to lift it.

"You're not going in the water with that on," he said, aghast.

"I'll be neutral in the water, like a jellyfish, so it helps me descend," George said, buckling it on. He plugged an air hose into his suit. "Besides, I can inflate the whole suit with this and bob to the surface like a balloon."

He picked up his mask, which was big enough to cover his nose and looked like giant goggles, and spat in it before rinsing it in the sea to keep it from fogging up. Next he put the mask over his face, slapped a gloved hand onto the sheathed knife on his leg, checked his watch and his gear bag containing the chart and waterproof clipboard, then rolled backward into the water with a mighty splash.

For a moment George floated on the surface, orienting himself. Then he looked up sharply at Jim, made a circle with the fingers of one hand, and, with a burst of bubbles, sank slowly beneath the waves.

Jim was suddenly alone in the beautiful, quiet inlet. The raucous laugh of a gull mocked him from a point he could not see. Oily smooth, the water seethed with a gentle swell that swished faintly over a nearby rock. A glorious sense of freedom and peace settled over him.

The water was so clear that thirty feet below, Jim could make out brown seaweed-covered ledges from which curtains of silver bubbles drifted slowly. George was setting out his grid on the sea floor. It was a full forty minutes before George surfaced, hissing and bloated like an ailing walrus. Jim was so relieved he could have hugged him, dry suit, tank, and all. George swam alongside and handed Jim the clipboard, specimen bag, and weight belt, and propelled himself out of the water with a powerful kick of his fins. He straddled the pontoon and swung his backpack and tank into the boat.

"Here's some supper," he said, spilling half a dozen rough reddish objects that looked like flat rocks from his specimen bag. "They have to be four inches across the shell to be legal size."

Jim turned one of them over and prodded the round leathery foot with his finger.

"They pay sixteen dollars a pound for that hunk of rubber?"

"It's a delicacy," said George.

Jim shrugged.

On the tenth day of diving, a fresh wind sprang up from the northwest. George was working a reef on the eastern tip of the Copper Islands and Jim was alone in the boat again. Gone were the blue skies and fluffy white clouds of the morning; in their place, gray layers of wet mist rolled down the mountains of South Moresby. Low cloud cover spat cold drops of rain across the rapidly building waves as Jim huddled in his orange floater suit waiting for George to surface. He checked his watch. George had been down thirty-five minutes and would be almost out of air. The friendly green of the sea had vanished, replaced by a somber steel color that chilled him to the core.

All of a sudden a ten-foot wave broke over the boat. Empty fuel cans sloshed about with the spare scuba tanks and their lunch bucket in the bottom of the boat. Jim decided not to wait any longer. He grabbed the hammer and pounded the steel bar underwater. Moments later, George's inflated head and shoulders broke the surface amid steep waves at least fifty yards downwind of the boat. George, a powerful swimmer, started to work his way back against the wind, but soon realized it was hopeless and raised his arm to be picked up.

His heart thumping wildly against his ribs, Jim started the motors, then went forward and hauled on the anchor. Nothing moved. A tinge of fear gripped his chest and he tugged frantically on the anchor line. Nothing. He could not pull the boat against the combined current and wind to get the anchor up. He looked back at George and saw that he was floating out into Hecate Strait, growing smaller by the second. Jim's knees started to shake.

"I've got to figure this out," Jim told himself. "Think!" Jim cried aloud. "Don't rush."

He set the propellers turning, then reached forward and pulled once more on the anchor line, pushing with his legs against the sponsons, gaining precious inches. But as soon as he reached for a further grip on the rope, the boat lurched back and the rope snapped taut. In a fury he screamed curses into the wind, tightened the belt on his floater suit, and hauled again with all his strength. Nothing. He put the props in neutral.

Jim looked back over his shoulder and for a sickening moment could not see George. Then, far out, a dark speck bobbed into view on the crest of a wave. In a flash, he remembered his father's knife. Fumbling in his pocket, he took out the knife and with one stroke parted the anchor line with a bang and the boat was free, blowing with the wind. Quickly, he engaged the props and moved the throttle forward, and the inflatable immediately plunged in the direction he had last seen George.

In his anxiety, Jim pushed the boat faster. Too fast. He grabbed a handgrip on the gunwale as the inflatable leapt off the edge of a wave. It struck the trough with a crash that threw him into the sloshing bilge. When he clambered to his feet, he was shaken, and had the coppery taste of blood in his mouth. But he scrambled to his seat, pulled back the throttle, and gripped the wheel again fiercely.

Soon, miraculously, the bulky head and shoulders of George appeared ahead.

"Always approach from downwind," Jim muttered as he swung the inflatable wide. "Not so fast. Not so fast." He eased back on the throttle.

He would not fail this time. He would not fail George. As he made the approach, he wished George had told him how to pick up a swimmer in such crazy waves.

George had turned to watch his approach. The inflatable bucked and rolled as Jim brought it across the ridges and gullies. He eased back more on the throttle, and before he knew it George was there, reaching for the boat. Jim hit neutral. With one hand George grabbed a rope loop on the gunwale, and with the other he tossed his weight belt and clipboard into the boat. A sudden wave pitched him sprawling into the bottom of the boat, and there he rested, face down in the sloshing bilge. Slowly he slipped out from beneath his scuba tank and reached back to open the self-draining plugs at the stern of the boat.

George then crawled forward to his seat, grinning weakly. "You're a good lad, Jim," he said. "Take her home."

The ride back to *King Fisher* that evening taught Jim another lesson about boat handling. The inflatable pounded across the waves, sometimes banging from crest to crest, at other times burrowing into the sides of waves and almost stopping in a wall of spray. Just as the waves were growing smaller and he was starting to relax, a gust of wind almost flipped them over as a squall forced itself beneath the lightweight boat. From then on, Jim watched keenly for the telltale spray of approaching gusts, and slowed down as they hit.

Aboard *King Fisher,* nothing was quite the same again for Jim. George told the story of his rescue and of Jim's boat handling and quick thinking. Jim sensed he had been tested and had measured up. A calm spot had started to grow inside him. Julia and Andreas, he noticed, treated him like he had at last become one of the crew.

ten

EVIDENCE
OF POACHERS

Over the next several days, as they worked Skincuttle Inlet, George found a few areas where the abalone were still large and plentiful, but these appeared to be places the poachers had missed. Most of the inlet had been picked clean, and when George dived these dead areas he grew angry.

"I can't believe how short-sighted people can be," he sputtered, blowing his nose after one dive and marking another zero onto the chart of Skincuttle Inlet. "They don't even leave anything to breed! This area has been virtually destroyed as abalone habitat for years."

One hot afternoon Jim and George returned to *King Fisher* early. Julia, who had finished her chores, was lying on the deck in the sunshine after a swim. "You should try it," she said. "The water is great."

Jim ran below and pulled on his swimsuit, and came back up. He stood balanced on the rail.

"Dive or jump?" she asked.

Jim did a neat header into the clear green water. The cold fairly took his breath away, and seemed to bore right into his head. He surfaced with a gasp. Julia sat on the rail, legs dangling, laughing mischievously.

"Cold, huh?"

Then, noticing something she had not seen before, she pointed to blotchy white patches on the bottom. "What's that white stuff?"

Jim retrieved a mask from the inflatable, which was tied alongside *King Fisher*. He was a strong swimmer and could go the length of a pool underwater, but this cold water was something new to him. He dived in again, fighting back the pain in his forehead. The water was clear and his heart missed a beat at the sight of the *King Fisher*'s hull, its propeller and rudder silhouetted darkly against the deep water. Down he kicked, until his ears hurt.

The bottom was still far away but it was close enough so he could see the shells—thousands of empty abalone shells. Long seconds later, he exploded at the surface and climbed aboard the inflatable.

"George! George!" he yelled. "There are zillions of abalone shells right underneath us!"

George, who had been cleaning his diving gear on deck, stepped down into the inflatable, put on the mask, and peered over the side.

"Good God," he said.

He hurried back onto *King Fisher,* only to return in a few moments, pulling on his dry suit. Soon he was fully kitted in the water with a fresh tank.

Jim and Julia watched as he sank to the bottom. For

fifteen minutes they followed the bubbles back and forth beneath the boat. Then George was up, passing Jim his gear. He pulled himself aboard and tore off his mask.

"Those bastards tied up to this very buoy and shucked mountains of abalone," he fumed. "They took everything, even the smallest ones."

Jim had never seen George so mad.

Throughout supper, George glowered. "I'd like to get my hands on the jerks who are destroying the ab stocks," he muttered. "What I really want to know is where they're based and how they are selling the undersized ones."

"What's so hard about selling undersized ones?" Jim asked.

"If they sold them through a fish packing plant, they'd be picked up by the inspectors," George said. "Canadian processing plants don't even buy shucked abalone. Retailers won't touch them."

"Maybe they aren't selling to Canadian buyers," Julia suggested.

"American ones are even stricter," he said.

"Hey, I know what's been happening," Jim joked. "A submarine sneaks in from Russia and picks them up."

"That may not be far from the truth," said George. "There have been reports of Korean fishing boats off the Queen Charlottes, but they usually stay well offshore."

When Jim came on deck the next morning, George was refueling the inflatable and loading up on extra gas. The scuba tanks were all back aboard the *King Fisher.*

"What's up?" Jim asked.

"I'm going to Rose Harbour to talk to Fisheries about nailing these guys," he said.

"Why don't you just use the radio?"

"Everyone and his dog listens in on channel 16."

"You want me?"

"No need. You stay here."

Jim considered his options for a moment.

"Is it okay if I borrow your kayak while you're gone, then?"

George hesitated. "I haven't shown you how to use it yet."

"I'll show him," Julia said eagerly.

George looked at Andreas. "What do you think?"

Andreas shrugged. "I'll keep an eye on them."

"Okay," said George, "but only go up the inlet. Don't go out to the Bolkus or Copper islands. Is that understood?"

"Yes sir!" Jim said, snapping his heels together and saluting.

"You know what I mean. I just don't want to have to go back to Vancouver and tell your mother I lost you."

eleven

KAYAKING TO
BURNABY NARROWS

As the departing inflatable became smaller in the distance, Julia and Jim eagerly turned over the kayaks and began the lessons. Julia retrieved two halves of a paddle and joined them together. The blades were long and narrow and didn't look to Jim like they would work very well. Julia assured him that they did. Piece by piece, she went through the equipment: the spray skirt that sealed the paddler into the tiny cockpit, the spare paddle, pump, and chart case. She pointed out the adjustable footrests and, still seated on the deck of *King Fisher,* showed Jim the correct way to sit and hold his elbows low, for the most relaxed stroke. Julia enjoyed teaching and it no longer bothered Jim so much.

When she had been through all the equipment, they lowered the kayaks into the water. Julia stepped nimbly into hers, sat down, and pushed off with her paddle. She floated gently away from *King Fisher,* adjusting her life jacket and attaching her spray skirt to the cockpit rim, and watched Jim climb unsteadily into the cockpit of George's kayak.

To Jim's relief, the kayak was very stable. As he floated away from the side of the boat, that delicious whiff of freedom swept over him again. He fumbled with his spray skirt, finally getting it in place, then looked over at Julia sitting in her kayak, independent and self-contained. They could go anywhere they wanted in these boats, he figured, and take everything they needed inside.

"You hold the paddle like this," Julia was saying, cradling the shaft lightly in a circle made with the thumb and forefinger of each hand. "Then you push with this hand while you pull with the other. Only the blade goes in the water."

"What about the rudder?" asked Jim.

"You use the rudder to hold your course in wind," she said. "Turn the kayak with the paddle and the angle of the boat, like this."

She swept the paddle wide while leaning the kayak far onto its side. All morning they practiced around Jedway Bay. In the shallows where the water was warmer, Julia demonstrated how to capsize the kayaks and how a paddle and a foam float attached to the end of the blade could serve as a stabilizing outrigger for reentering the boat. When they returned to *King Fisher*, Andreas made them both capsize and reenter in deep, cold water.

"Not bad," he admitted as they climbed aboard, shivering.

"Can we go exploring after lunch?" Julia pleaded.

"You always said I couldn't go alone. Now I won't be alone!"

Andreas smiled. "You can go up Huston Inlet as long as you take all the proper safety gear."

Andreas always claimed he believed taking risks was part of learning about life, but he still had trouble when it came to his own daughter. Kids, he knew, were usually fine when they were taught well, then given enough responsibility. Even so, he fussed about as they prepared to leave. He had them assemble their equipment on deck, and he looked it over critically. Two waterproof bags with emergency food and dry clothing were closed tightly.

"Be sure to take the bear spray," said Andreas. "There are plenty of black bears here."

"What's bear spray?" Jim asked.

Julia opened a drawer in the wheelhouse and removed a canister that looked like a small fire extinguisher. "You take off that safety catch and press," she said. "It sprays a pepper solution that will drive a bear away." Then she slipped it into a holster and put it in her bag.

"You're kidding."

"You always think people are kidding," she said, smiling.

"Have you each got matches and a knife?" Andreas asked.

They both said yes.

He picked up the emergency bag George had left with the kayak. "Do you know how to work these?" Andreas said, pulling out a flare and flicking off the plastic cap at one end.

"Those are emergency flares," Jim answered. "When you need help, hold it at arm's length and pull the string and it will send up a glowing flare. George showed me."

"Right," Andreas said. Then he pulled out a small card compass with a long loop of string. "This goes around your neck," he added, putting it over Julia's head.

Then Jim and Julia transferred the gear to the skiff, and loaded it into the kayaks which were floating next to it. The bags were stowed in watertight areas fore and aft of the cockpit, and they then sealed the hatches with waterproof gaskets.

After lunch, the two set off in their kayaks. A light wind followed them as they rounded a small wooded island at the entrance to Jedway Bay and turned south, along the eastern shore of Huston Inlet. The water was as smooth as glass and the air was quiet away from the throb of the *King Fisher*'s generator. They cruised side by side just outside the kelp beds, savoring the stillness and playing tag with a brilliant blue kingfisher that swooped from rock to rock ahead of them.

To their left, a wall of dark rock rose steeply from the sea. Rolls of thick green moss and tangled roots spilled over from the forest. At first, Jim found it uncomfortable to have his legs stretched out in front of him, but then he discovered that if he locked his knees under the deck with his feet snug against the footrests, the kayak felt like it was part of him and he had no trouble with cramping. He learned to adjust his balance with a flick of his hips as if he were wearing the boat, and through its movement he could feel every twist and turn of the sea. His paddle began to feel like an extension of his hands—hands that could pull through the water or offer support and stability or send a shower of spray over Julia.

It took an hour to reach the head of Huston Inlet. They pulled the kayaks onto the beach, and gulped handfuls of cool water scooped from a shallow stream that splashed down over mossy rocks. Above a stand of tall spruce, a bald eagle watched them from a snag. It was the first time Jim had seen one up close: he could even see the powerful yellow talons and curved beak. He was relieved to see that the eagle was anything but bald. In fact it had a fine head of white plumage. Farther along the shore, statuesque, a great blue heron stood poised to strike unwary small fish in the shallows.

As they were eating a snack of dried fruit and chocolate, swarms of mosquitoes found them and began a feast of their own. Julia and Jim bolted for their kayaks, swatting wildly at the cloud with their jackets. Continuing around the head of the inlet, they started up the western shore. By then it was six o'clock, and the forested slopes to their left were steeped in shadow as the sun dropped behind the mountains. Ahead of them, low over the water, the heron flapped with slow graceful strokes through the hazy shadows to the edge of its territory, then doubled back in a wide half circle.

Back at the entrance to Huston Inlet, they could see *King Fisher* a mile away, bathed in pale reflected light from the sky. A chill wind whisked up a small chop from the north as Jim and Julia set their course for home.

That evening they ate a late supper, expecting George at any time.

"Must be staying the night," Andreas said eventually.

"We paddled ten miles today," announced Julia, who had been poring over the chart on the galley table. "Pretty good, eh?"

"Pretty good," Andreas agreed.

"Can we go to Burnaby Narrows tomorrow?" asked Julia.

"That's okay with me as long as the weather . . . Shhh!" whispered Andreas, holding up his hand.

Jim listened to the drone of the generator. Andreas stepped outside, followed closely by the others.

"What is it?" asked Julia.

"I thought I heard a motor. Sometimes you can sense a propeller when you're inside a boat, even when you can't hear the motor outside."

"I think I hear something now," said Jim.

"It must be George," Julia decided.

"No. It's the wrong sound for the inflatable," Andreas said. He turned off the generator and the lights dimmed as they switched automatically to the battery. In the abrupt silence, the faint throb of a diesel motor floated across the still waters.

"It seems to be directly in front of us," Julia observed.

"Must be just beyond the islands," Andreas said, "or else they are traveling without lights."

The three stood peering into the darkness, listening to the receding motor.

"I've never seen so many stars," Jim said, looking up. "Hey! Did you see that shooting star?"

"Make a wish," said Julia.

Jim closed his eyes and wished that George would make it back safely.

"What did you wish?" asked Julia.

"Can't tell or it won't happen," said Jim.

"From the sound of it, that boat was going up the inlet," said Andreas, wrinkling his brows.

When Jim awoke the next morning, a bright circle of sunlight was moving erratically across George's empty bunk as *King Fisher* swung gently at her mooring. On deck, the chill was being driven from the air by the sun, already burning off the heavy dew. Mist rose from the forest, carved into slanting columns by the sun's rays angling through the trees. Across the inlet, eagles circled and a sea lion broke the glassy surface and then dove again as it pursued a fish. Julia had her kayak across the rail and was sponging water from the cockpit, while Andreas bailed the old aluminum skiff.

Jim stretched. "Ouch!" he cried.

"You sore too?" asked Julia. "I could hardly get out of bed this morning."

Jim sat down on a fuel drum and continued the process of waking up. "Have you heard from George?" he asked.

"Yes. He called on the radio after you went to bed. Said he was going to try to make it back tonight."

"That gives us the whole day! Let's hit the water then," Jim said abruptly.

After breakfast, Jim and Julia loaded their gear and shoved off.

Jim checked his watch as the two kayaks drifted clear of *King Fisher*. It was eight thirty. Muscles screamed in protest as the paddlers started out, but gradually they limbered up, and the clear green water began to slip by.

They retraced the final crossing of the previous

evening and, by nine o'clock, had arrived at the low wooded headland at the far side of Huston Inlet and a shallow estuary marked on their chart as Slim Inlet. The sea was smooth with only the lightest puffs of air, so they headed directly north across Skincuttle Inlet to the southern tip of Burnaby Island. It was their longest crossing yet, and in the middle, fully a mile from land, they stopped and drifted to gaze about while a curious sea lion cruised back and forth some twenty feet ahead, snorting with indignation at the intrusion.

As they watched, the huge sea lion dived and a curved wave sped across in front of them, bursting suddenly in a flash of silver and brown with pink flecks of blood as the sea lion caught a fine salmon. It lifted the big fish clear out of the water and snapped it back and forth, tearing a huge chunk out of its belly. From nowhere, a group of gulls pounced screeching, and hovered above the sea lion, dipping to pick up stray morsels.

They drew their kayaks together and watched the duel over the salmon. Jim passed over a piece of gum, and they swigged water from the bottle Julia carried on deck.

"Wouldn't you like to live here?" she said.

"I'd like to build a house over there and only go to town once a month," said Jim, pointing to a white beach with bright green grass behind it.

"Once a year would suit me," Julia said. "I sometimes wish I didn't have to go back to town. I never seem to get used to that part of my life. It doesn't seem real."

Jim scooped up some floating seaweed with his hand and watched the sunlight pass through it, turning it the color of maple syrup. "How come your mother doesn't work on the boat too?" he asked.

"My mother!" Julia exclaimed. "She won't go near the *King Fisher* while my dad is on board. They don't get along these days."

"Oh, that's too bad," said Jim.

Julia looked at him with a strange expression he hadn't seen before. "She used to work the boat with him—before I was born. I guess I messed up a good thing. They started to fight, so now I get to spend summers with my dad and the rest of the year with my mom."

The sea lion appeared again, taking one last swipe at the floating fish. It came high out of the water, looking around, long whiskers atwitch, eyes like big glossy black marbles.

"Are your mom and dad separated too?" Julia asked.

Jim stared out to sea. "You might call it that," he said. "My dad was killed in a car accident two years ago. A drunk driver crossed the centerline and crashed into us head-on. Dad died instantly. The drunk staggered away with a few scratches. I broke my wrist."

"Oh, I'm sorry," Julia said awkwardly.

The old knot had returned to Jim's stomach. He blinked back tears, embarrassed that he still choked up so quickly about it after so much time. "I hate drunks," he said thickly.

The water grew shallow near Dolomite Narrows, a magical place where two forested peninsulas almost met over hundreds of acres of knee-deep shallows. The rising tide that carried them forward floated clam shells off the shore like little porcelain boats. Jim and Julia could reach down and touch huge squishy sea stars—orange, purple, red—that prowled the stony bottom hunting for unwary mollusks, while along the shore, shiny black oystercatchers with bright orange beaks rushed about like kids on a treasure hunt.

At the narrowest point they stepped out of their kayaks and dragged them onto a pebble beach near an abandoned log cabin.

"We're not the only ones who want to live here," observed Jim.

They gathered dry wood, and Jim lit a fire beside a large smooth rock. He skewered hot dogs on sharpened alder sticks and sat roasting them while Julia waded the shallows, searching the bottom with her hands.

"Come and get it!" yelled Jim, when the hot dogs wore a healthy crust of charcoal. Julia returned and set six large wet clams down in the hot coals.

"We should have brought lemon," she said. "Then they'd be perfect."

They sat on the warm beach stones and ate, trying to avoid the smoke that seemed to follow them around.

"Look!" Jim said, pointing to a small black-tailed deer delicately picking its way along the edge of the forest.

"There are too many deer on the Queen Charlottes," said Julia. "They were introduced from the mainland and now they are eating all the little trees so the forests can't grow. They have no predators here, except man and sometimes bears."

"What about wolves?"

"No wolves in the Queen Charlottes."

"Don't you think it's crazy the way people screw up every time they meddle with nature?" Jim said. "Just like the abalone." He picked up a bleached abalone shell and turned it over in his hand. "It's so rough on the outside, and so smooth and pretty on the inside. And we kill millions of them because they are valuable."

"It sounds funny to hear you talk like that."

"What's funny about it?"

"Well, I sort of expected you to be going around breaking everything up," she said.

Jim looked alarmed.

"Is that what they told you?"

"Well, not exactly. Dad just said you were a pretty wild city kid. I'm surprised you care about these things."

"Me, too," Jim admitted. "I guess I never thought about them before."

The deer had stopped at the sound of their voices, its huge ears cocked forward as it sniffed the air. Apparently satisfied that the surprise visitors were harmless, it continued along the beach, then reentered the forest.

When the clam shells opened, Julia took them out of the coals with a forked stick and pushed one toward Jim. He blew on it, then scooped the plump flesh from the hot shell with the blade of his knife.

"You drink the juice too," said Julia, slurping from the shell.

They skipped the empties across the narrow channel.

twelve

THE *DARK SABLE*

After lunch, they explored the abandoned cabin at the edge of the forest. Inside the gloomy structure, broken furniture was covered with mouse droppings, while behind the cabin they found the fresh prints of a very large bear. Judging from the number of tracks, it was clear the cabin was one of the bruin's favorite haunts. Looking at each other, they needed no discussion. Hastily, they returned to the kayaks, dragged them to the water, and headed back along the eastern shore of Moresby.

Their return journey was eased by a following breeze which nudged them along with a friendly escort of wavelets. They nosed their kayaks into coves and around kelp-covered rocks, and explored streams of crystal-clear water until overhanging branches or boulders barred their way. At the entrance to Slim Inlet, Julia paused and studied the chart.

"Let's see what's at the end," she said. "It's not far."

Jim looked at his watch: three o'clock. He loved these northern summers. It wouldn't get dark until after ten. "Sure, let's go!"

As they paddled up Slim Inlet, the channel narrowed to a stone's throw. A final twist brought them to a cul-de-sac where trees overhung the water and three small streams met the sea. They leaned on their backrests and let their kayaks drift under curtains of moss. Jim gave two more strokes, then turned his kayak into the largest of the streams.

Suddenly, he stiffened. There, tucked against the bank, lay *Dark Sable,* almost hidden beneath a camouflage net laced with strips of brown and green cloth. Jim backpaddled hastily.

"It's them. It's the poachers!" he whispered.

A look of disbelief crossed Julia's face. Cautiously she edged forward. Her jaw dropped and she backpaddled as quietly as she could, then brought her kayak around and took off after Jim, who was headed full speed down Slim Inlet. Jim paused to let her catch up.

"What should we do?" he whispered.

"We should tell George," Julia whispered back, her voice quivering with excitement.

"He's not back yet. Maybe we could creep up and have a closer look," Jim suggested. "Hide the kayaks and sneak through the trees."

Julia considered for a moment. Certainly it would be helpful to know more about the poachers' base before they raised the alarm. "We'll have to be careful no one sees us."

They paddled to the rocky east shore, then, taking an

end each, carried the kayaks one at a time into the forest and slid them under the salal bushes. Stowing their paddles and life jackets under the boats, they collected branches and moss to further camouflage the boats.

"You'd have to bump into them before you saw them," Jim said proudly when they had finished.

Jim quickly loaded his day pack with snack food and George's emergency kit, and as an afterthought tossed in the flashlight. Julia threaded the bear spray holster onto her belt and stuffed the map up her sweater. Both rubbed mosquito repellent on exposed skin and then they were ready.

Together, they set off pushing through the thick salal. Progress was noisy and slow at first, but the stiff bushes soon gave way to a tangle of medium-sized trees with spindly underbrush. As they neared the head of the inlet, where they had spotted *Dark Sable,* the trees became shorter and thicker and the ground flat and swampy. Frustrated mosquitoes crowded their mouths and eyes.

"The deer have done that," whispered Julia, pointing to the forest of stunted, prickly trees. Most rose no higher than their heads, and in places they grew so densely that the deer themselves had to push their way through, creating tunnels just the right size for a kid.

While following one of these trails, sometimes standing, sometimes scrambling on all fours with the pack in tow, they came upon a stream that moved slowly over smooth, round boulders. Beside it was a wide, well-worn track marked by a broad line of small, square imprints.

"That's from an ATV," Jim whispered.

Julia wrinkled her brow.

"An all-terrain vehicle," Jim explained. "You know, those baby tractors with fat tires. They can drive through almost anything, even swamp."

They turned right on the trail. Within a hundred yards, they spied the *Dark Sable*. Ducking into one of the convenient tunnels in the bushes, they watched and waited. There was no sound but the gurgle of water and the buzz of mosquitoes.

"There doesn't seem to be anyone on board," Julia whispered. Cautiously, they drew closer to the boat.

"Look over there," Jim said softly, pointing to a rough cedar shed. The door was padlocked and chained. An aluminum skiff was propped against the back of the structure. Walking over to the shed, they pressed their noses to a crack.

"Got the flashlight?" whispered Julia. Jim shone his light through the tiny gap, and inside they could see an outboard engine, rows of scuba tanks, and some silver-painted machinery.

"That's their compressor," said Julia. "But where do they put the abalone?"

"On the boat maybe?"

"No. The boat's too small. They have to store it some-place."

"Maybe we should follow the trail," suggested Jim, halfheartedly. He didn't like the thought of coming face to face with the big tattooed man.

"Yes, let's," said Julia.

They set off, sneaking along the edge of the trail, trying not to make any footprints in the soft ground, and ready, at the first sign of danger, to dive into one of the deer tunnels. In places where the trail plunged into swamps, they took to the tunnels, and skirted wide to help hide their footprints. They passed a small lake studded with low islands of emerald green sphagnum moss, and beyond it the trail continued its gentle rise to drier ground. A quarter of a mile farther, the path dipped past another small lake surrounded by swamp, then back to the stream once more.

"Wait a minute," Jim said suddenly. "There's something weird about that stream."

Julia looked at it and shrugged.

"It's going the same way as we are," he said. "The last one was going the other way."

"So?"

"Do you think we've gone in a circle and are heading back down again?"

"That couldn't be," said Julia. She reached for the compass around her neck, and they both looked at it.

"No, we're still heading south," Jim said, puzzled.

Julia pulled the chart of South Moresby from inside her sweater and spread it out on a mound of moss.

"Look," she said. "The trail must lead down to Louscoone Inlet. This must be a different stream, flowing down to the west side of the island."

"Louscoone Inlet is on the west coast of Moresby!" Jim exclaimed. "So that's how they take out the abalone! Fisheries would never think to look there!"

Walking faster, they followed the stream down, past a feeder creek that bounced down the hillside to their left. Across the valley they could see sparsely forested slopes rolling up toward the setting sun.

They had gone about half a mile and had just passed a second stream when Jim froze.

"Shhh!" he said. "I hear voices."

They dove into the nearest tunnel, their hearts pounding. Julia crawled up beside Jim and slipped the bear spray out of its sheath. Through the thick branches of the bushes they could see two men wearing gum boots and dirty yellow raingear, striding down the streambed Jim and Julia had just crossed.

Jim gave a quiet moan. "It's the big guy with the tattoos," he whispered.

When the men reached the path, they turned and walked straight toward where Jim and Julia were hiding. Jim held his breath, listening to the thud and squelch of heavy boots on the trail and the pulse pounding in his ears.

"We'll start moving 'em out tomorrow night, eh," the tattooed man was saying.

"I sure would like to see it full," said his companion.

"It's too risky, eh," said the tattooed man. "We can't go out again with that damn research boat at Jedway. Besides, Fujita's getting jumpy. He doesn't like getting so close to shore."

"Well, he's gonna have to get used to it if he wants the abs. We're gettin' real low on gas, and there's no way we can take them out ten miles for him," said the second man.

The voices faded abruptly as the path to Louscoone Inlet took a turn. Jim and Julia scarcely breathed for several minutes. They remained crouched, tense, listening for voices or footsteps. Julia was the first to break the spell. She slipped the bear spray back into its holster and crept out of their tunnel.

"There must be something up that stream," she

whispered. Together they walked back and examined the creekbed, poised to dive for cover at the slightest sound.

"Yes, look," said Jim. "There's a tire mark on the edge of this bank. Clever. By using the streambed as their trail, their ATV hardly leaves any tracks."

Jim and Julia stepped from one smooth wet boulder to another, following the stream uphill. All of a sudden they came upon a large square building painted a dull green and camouflaged with netting, moss, and branches. As they approached, the purr of a well-muffled motor rose above the splash of the stream.

"It's a freezer," said Julia, slipping the bear spray out of its holster. "We've found where they keep the abalone!"

Next to the building, a fifty-gallon fuel drum sat on a cradle and a stack of freezer trays leaned against the wall.

"They said they were short of fuel," said Jim. "How about we make them a little shorter?" He turned on the tap and gasoline splashed onto the ground.

"That's bad for the environment," said Julia.

"It's just gas. We used to make bottle bombs with this stuff. It evaporates fast." He turned the flow down to a trickle.

"They'll kill us if they know we did that," Julia said, looking around frantically.

"How will they know?"

Reluctantly, Julia followed Jim toward the freezer.

"You'd better stand watch," said Jim. "I'll go in."

He tried the door but it was locked. Quickly he looked about for likely places to hide a key, first lifting a piece of wood, then a nearby brick. "Aha," he said, "people always leave keys in such obvious places."

"You look like you've done this before," Julia observed.

"Just keep a good watch. You won't hear someone coming above the sound of the motor," he warned, fitting the key in the lock.

The lock clunked open and Jim pushed the door open and stepped in, flashlight in hand. The freezing air bit through his clothing. Piled almost to the roof were dozens of plastic sacks of frozen, shucked abalone. Freezing racks loaded with more abalone in the process of being glazed with brine stood across from a large fan on the left side. He picked a rock-hard undersized abalone off the shelf, then went outside and showed it to Julia.

"Let's go," she pleaded.

Carefully Jim locked the door and replaced the key. Then he looked over the ground, patting down and disguising any sign of their visit.

"Why bother?" said Julia. "They'll know someone was here when they find the fuel gone."

Jim walked over to the drum and opened the tap to more of a dribble. "I think they'll both think the other one left it on if they don't find our tracks," he said.

Jim led the way back down the stream, intent on picking up the trail to Louscoone. Before they reached it, he changed his mind and entered a tunnel that struck off across the hillside, parallel to and about fifty yards above the main trail. Every twenty feet or so the tunnel roof opened up so they could look over the well-nibbled bushes and see the main trail below them.

They had gone almost a quarter of a mile when they came upon another stream. Near its intersection with the main trail stood a cabin, well hidden beneath some trees. Smoke drifted from the chimney. The ATV, trailer attached, was parked near the cabin, while nearby, in the tidal waters of the stream, a sleek speedboat peeked out from beneath its camouflaged cover. To the south, Louscoone Inlet stretched like a silver road to the Pacific Ocean.

"Let's go back," whispered Julia.

"There's another drum of gas," said Jim quietly, pointing to the stream bank near the speedboat.

"It's getting late."

"I'll be quick!"

Jim took off his pack and handed it to Julia. Bending down, he disappeared into a tunnel that led downhill. He crawled on his belly for the last twenty feet, wondering why he was sticking his neck out like this. It would have been much smarter just to head back like Julia suggested. He slithered to within six feet of the drum, with only a thin wall of salal between him and his objective. Slowly he pushed through the foliage, certain the whole world could hear the rustling. Julia, still hidden in the bushes on the hillside, could hardly bear to watch as she saw Jim's hand emerge from the foliage and turn the tap. Gas first gushed onto the gravel and then Jim slowed the flow to a trickle.

Suddenly a man with a black bushy beard burst into the open from the direction of *Dark Sable*. Jim's heart nearly stopped as he backed frantically into the salal.

"Someone's been snooping 'round the boat," the man yelled.

The cabin door swung open just as the bearded man

reached for the door handle and collided with the tattooed man. Three more men, including the ones they had seen walking back from the freezer, came rushing out of the cabin.

"What are you telling me?" the tattooed man boomed.

"Footprints around the storage shed. Small prints, like kids'."

The tattooed hulk went inside the cabin and reappeared with a hunting rifle.

"I'll put a stop to snoopers," he said grimly. Suddenly he turned and sniffed the air.

"I smell gas." He glared at his companions.

"I refueled the four-wheeler about half an hour ago, boss," said a blond man with a bushy red beard. The tattooed man moved toward the boat, his nose twitching.

"You idiot!" he bellowed. "You left the tap on!"

He lunged for the tap barely three feet from where Jim crouched, then turned on his companions. Jim didn't breathe. For the second time that afternoon, he heard his pulse pounding in his ears.

"I should shoot you for that," he snarled. "But that would be too kind."

Jim braced himself, half expecting the grip of that powerful tattooed hand on his shoulder.

"But boss, I didn't leave it on," the man whined.

"Then who the hell did?" roared the tattooed man, gesturing to the forest where Julia lay. "A Sasquatch?"

"I don't know, boss, but it wasn't me."

"Get out of my sight," the big man sneered. "On second thought, you go find those snoopers and bring them here. We'll put them out of the way until we leave."

The red-bearded man reached for the rifle.

"No way," snarled his boss. "I wouldn't trust you with a gun. Take a club, you Neanderthal."

All the men went into the cabin except for redbeard, who picked up a sturdy stick and set off down the trail, muttering to himself. Jim waited a few seconds, then reached out cautiously and turned the tap back on to a trickle. Retracing his steps, he scrambled back up the hillside to where Julia crouched, waiting.

"You're crazy," she hissed.

"Let's get outta here!" Jim gasped. He checked his watch: nine o'clock already!

thirteen

PEPPER

We need to go northwest along the hillside," Jim announced, looking at Julia's compass to get oriented. "Not a chance of using the main trail."

The compass needle shook uncontrollably in his hand as they moved up the hill. Their route followed a high arc where the trees grew taller and the going was more open. Jim picked up a sturdy stick, and Julia held the bear spray in her hand, safety catch backed off one notch. When they spoke, they did so in whispers, mindful that somewhere below or perhaps in front, the man with the red beard was hunting for them.

The sun had long since fallen behind the mountains, and a gloom settled over the forest. Moss hung from the trees, assuming grotesque shapes. In some places, the underbrush was so thick they couldn't get through and had to detour and pick up another game trail. At one point in the growing darkness, Jim started and almost clubbed a mossy stump: it looked exactly like the crouched form of a man.

They passed the second lake, keeping to the edge of the main path once the game trails became too dark. Soon they were approaching the *Dark Sable,* and began searching for the trail leading to their kayaks. Mosquitoes flung themselves at their faces in a frenzy, and Jim breathed one in and began coughing. Suddenly, one of the mossy forms reared up.

"Gotcha! Ya little rats," it snarled.

Jim bolted as redbeard rushed them. But Julia stood her ground.

"Run!" Jim yelled, hesitating. The man was ten feet from Julia, club raised, when Jim heard a *whoosh.* Redbeard crumpled to the ground, writhing, his hands clutching his face as he squirmed in the dirt, moaning. Julia stood, feet apart, the bear spray still held up at eye level with both hands shaking wildly.

"Holy smoke," said Jim, approaching cautiously. "Look what you did to him!"

Suddenly they were both coughing. A burning pain seized their throats and eyes.

"Let's get away from here," Jim said, tugging on Julia's sleeve.

"The safety. I need the safety." She fumbled on the ground. "Got it," she said triumphantly. Julia was beginning to shake all over. Jim took her by the arm and dragged her away from the thrashing, wheezing man.

"Is he going to die?" whispered Jim.

"No. It only lasts for half an hour, then he'll be okay," said Julia, coughing.

Tears streamed from their burning eyes as they

crashed their way through the stunted forest. Passing a small creek, they paused and splashed water into their faces.

"And we only got a whiff of it," marveled Jim. "That stuff is ferocious."

"It'll stop a grizzly," said Julia.

"I believe it."

They found the kayaks as they had left them and dragged them down to the channel, which had become much narrower as the tide had fallen.

"If you're right about that stuff lasting half an hour, that guy will be okay in about fifteen minutes," said Jim. "Chances are he'll be after us in the skiff."

They paddled hard. Green sky silhouetted the mountains of South Moresby. Stars twinkled in the east. As they rounded the headland before Huston Inlet, the light of a campfire on shore greeted them. Kayaks were drawn up on the beach and people milled about brightly colored tents. It looked so friendly and safe.

"Maybe old redbeard will think we came from that tour group if he comes out this way," said Jim.

"He'll think twice before attacking them with his club, anyway," Julia said, with a giggle.

They were midway across Huston Inlet and paddling steadily when, for a few moments, the sound of an outboard engine reached them. But night had drawn its dark cloak over them and they moved on confidently into a gentle northwest wind, paddling side by side along a trail of reflections that danced toward them from the lights aboard *King Fisher*.

fourteen

THE PLAN

The kayaks glided between the islands at the entrance to Jedway Bay and slid alongside the fishing boat.

Jim's heart jumped when he saw the inflatable.

"Ahoy! Anyone home?" he called.

Two heads appeared over the rail, above them.

"Thank God you're back," said George angrily. "What on earth have you been up to?"

"We've been visiting the *Dark Sable* guys," said Jim.

"Just look at yourselves," said Andreas.

They climbed aboard. Jim was shocked to see how filthy Julia looked. But comparing arms and legs, they discovered they were equally dirty and covered with scratches, and their hair was tangled with leaves and twigs. After washing up, they told their story over hot bowls of fish stew and surrounded by the cozy smells of the galley. And gradually the anger on the faces of Andreas and George turned to amazement.

"Chances are they will think that party of kayakers was responsible when they see the drag marks on the beach in the morning," said George. "That means we probably still have the benefit of surprise."

"Not much time to do anything if they're moving the abalone tomorrow night," Andreas said doubtfully.

"Can't you just arrest them in the morning?" Jim asked. "We know where the evidence is now."

"We could, thanks to you and Julia," said George. "But we have a chance to catch the big boy this time."

"Tex was flying over the coast the other day and saw a deep-sea trawler about twelve miles offshore, and I'll bet that's our man," said Andreas.

"Fujita?" Jim asked.

"Exactly. And since the poachers are now really short of fuel, the pickup ship will almost certainly have to come in close. Then all of them can be arrested."

After Jim and Julia had gone to bed, Andreas switched on the marine radio and George took out a chart tube and a pad of paper he'd brought back from Rose Harbour. During his visit with Fisheries, he had established a simple radio code so the poachers, if they were listening, would not be tipped off by any conversations he might have with Fisheries. It went like this:

groceries = abalone	taxi = helicopter
mother = buyer	seiner = Coast Guard
oyster = *King Fisher*	gillnetter = Fisheries
tourists = poachers	father = police

George took a sheet of tracing paper out of the tube. On it was a grid with numbers written across the top and down one side. The Fisheries and Coast Guard vessels each had an identical grid. He took chart 3853 from a drawer in the wheelhouse, then carefully taped the transparent paper on top of it so the bottom right-hand corner of the grid matched the bottom right-hand corner of the chart. Before they went to bed, Julia and Jim had marked the positions of the cabin, freezer, and *Dark Sable* on the chart. Now George was able to record the codes for the location of all these positions on a notepad.

"Switch to channel 51," George said.

Andreas looked at him sideways. "No one stands by on 51," he said.

"Precisely."

The speaker hissed gently.

"Gillnetter, this is oyster. Do you read? Over."

"Oyster, this is gillnetter. Over," came the prompt response.

"Well, I'll be darned," muttered Andreas.

"The tourists are camped at forty-two sixty-one, and it seems mother wants the groceries delivered tomorrow night. Over." There was a pause.

"Understood. The tourists are delivering groceries to mother tomorrow night," the radio crackled.

"Roger. Have the taxi pick me up at oyster at zero six hundred hours, and I'll coordinate from forty-five eighty-four. Over."

George leaned back and grinned. "That should make 'em scratch their heads if they're listening," he chuckled.

Jim woke to the pulse of the helicopter rotors directly above *King Fisher*. He sprang out of his bunk, pulled on his clothes, and collided with Julia in the passageway.

Together they ran up on deck. From there they could watch as Tex settled the chopper on the gravel beach a hundred yards away. George was already on his way to pick him up in the inflatable.

"Well, howdy," said Tex as he climbed on board *King Fisher*. "You enjoyin' life on a fishing boat, young fella?"

Jim grinned awkwardly.

Tex turned to Julia and squeezed her shoulders in a friendly hug. "You keepin' him in line now?" he said. "These city boys need someone to make sure they don't get into no trouble."

"No kidding!" said Julia with a sidelong glance at Jim.

"See, you didn't need to worry. She's pretty cool, huh?" Tex said, turning back to Jim.

Jim felt his face turning red. "Pretty cool with the bear spray," he answered.

Andreas laughed, and Tex looked puzzled. Everyone trooped below and sat around the galley table while George filled Tex in on the previous day's adventures. Jim and Julia each munched a bowl of cereal while the men drank coffee. Tex whistled when he heard of the encounter with redbeard.

"I see what you mean," he said to Jim. "Don't mess with Big Julie, huh?" Then Tex turned to George. "So what's the plan now?" he asked.

"Well, I reckon I go with you to set things up with Fisheries at Rose Harbour. The Coast Guard has a cutter off Cape St. James at the southern tip of Moresby. It's most unlikely the buyer will come in during daylight. That leaves them with only five or six hours of darkness to get in, load the abalone, then get back out to sea. I think we should wait until they have one load aboard, then make our move. The *King Fisher* can stay here and keep *Dark Sable* bottled up in Slim Inlet or follow her if she makes a break."

Tex put his chin in his hand and looked critically at the chart.

"How're you gonna stop a deep-sea trawler?" he asked. "She's as big as a midsize ferryboat, you know, and a lot faster."

"That'll be up to the Coast Guard," said George.

Tex shook his head and screwed up his nose disapprovingly.

"All due respect to Her Majesty's Coast Guard," he said, "but I wouldn't count on 'em. What if Mister Whatsisname decides to keep going, which I certainly would if I was him? How y'all gonna stop him?"

"Blow him out of the water," said Jim enthusiastically.

Tex gave him a gentle punch to the shoulder. "We're talking Canadian Coast Guard here, not American," he said. "These boys will run alongside talking to Whatsisname till he's outside the two-hundred-mile limit. Then they'll go home and write a report."

"Well, what do you suggest?" said George.

Tex winked at Jim. "Catch 'em yourself. For a start, you better forget about coming with me. Your best bet would be to get over to Anthony Island with the inflatable," he said to George. "Then you can use a trick the Viet Cong pulled to stop our patrol boats in 'Nam."

fifteen

SETTING A TRAP

Half an hour later, Tex was lifting off into the air, leaving the crew of *King Fisher* outfitting the inflatable for a long trip. When available fuel tanks were stowed aboard, Andreas hauled two hundred yards of one-inch polypropylene floating rope out of the hold and coiled it into the bottom of the inflatable. George took a duffel bag and loaded it with an assortment of canned food and some bread from the freezer.

"I'm coming with you for sure this time," Jim announced determinedly.

"Too dangerous," George answered.

"It will be dangerous trying to block the *Dark Sable*, too," Jim pointed out. "Besides, you are going to need help and we're a team, right?"

George looked at his eager face and reconsidered. "Okay," he finally agreed, "but you may have to stay on the Fisheries protection boat. Get some warm clothes, your sleeping bag, and your floater suit, and be quick."

"May I come too?" Julia pleaded, jumping up and down.

"I'll need you here," Andreas said firmly.

"Ohhh!" she groaned.

"If *Dark Sable* makes a run for it, you'll have plenty of excitement," said George.

Soon after eight, Jim and George were ready to go. Jim started the inflatable's motors and George cast off, then sat down heavily. Jim eased forward on the throttle, and the inflatable surged sluggishly up to planing speed. Looking back, Jim could see Andreas and Julia waving from the *King Fisher*. He felt good, and a thrill of excitement ran through him as he gripped the wheel.

For the first five miles, they headed east, skimming the south shore of Skincuttle Inlet about fifty yards out from the rocks. Gradually the land curved south, rolling back from the coast in folds of dark, thick forest. They were in Hecate Strait. The day was beginning to warm up, but on the sea the breeze was cool as they sped over long, low swells rolling in from the south.

"That's Collision Bay," yelled George, pointing into a calm harbor to starboard. "It was quite a settlement in its day. They used to take oceangoing ships in there to load copper ore."

Jim stared, expecting to see cabins and maybe derelict railroad cars, but could see only trees.

"You can still find twisted railroad track and rusty cable in the trees," George explained. "Nobody knows how to find all the old mines now. The forest has taken them back."

A northwesterly breeze sprang up as they crossed the

broad entrance to Carpenter Bay. Once across, George pointed out a shortcut that skipped inside some rocky islands to which gnarled, stunted trees clung hopefully. More kayakers were putting to sea as they rounded Benjamin Point. The colorful boats looked pretty in the early morning sunlight, and Jim thought he should return to this spot with Julia in their kayaks soon.

"There's a big black bear living here," said George, gesturing at the point. "They call her Benjie. She's good at chasing the kayakers away from their food, so she can help herself."

Jim caught himself grinning. It felt so good to be out on the open sea at the wheel of a fast boat with George. Wind tugged his hair. He swung the wheel and the deep V of the boat bit into the ocean, sending a curtain of water into the air.

"Hey, steady there," said George halfheartedly.

Jim just kept grinning.

The seas calmed as they entered the passage between Moresby and Kunghit islands. The gray Fisheries vessel lurked behind a small rocky island that had a settlement of old houses.

"Rose Harbour," said George.

As Julia watched the inflatable depart, a hollow feeling settled inside her. "It's not fair that they should have all the fun," she grumbled.

"They won't," her father said.

Andreas went below, soon reappearing with four plastic bags, a necklace of heavy shackles, and a roll of five-eighths-inch polypropylene floating rope.

"Here," he said. "Help me make these boat snares."

"Boat snares?"

"They'll float across the channel and wrap around the propellers."

As Julia watched, her dad fastened one end of the rope to a shackle and dropped it into a plastic bag, then measured and stuffed a hundred yards of rope into the bag, followed by a second shackle attached to the other end of the rope.

When four such bags had been prepared, Andreas and Julia slipped *King Fisher*'s mooring and motored across the mouth of Huston Inlet, dropping anchor off the point just at the entrance to Slim Inlet where Julia and Jim had seen the kayakers camped the previous night.

The campsite was deserted. Andreas and Julia lowered their own kayaks into the calm waters and, taking two rope bags each, paddled stealthily up Slim Inlet to its narrowest part, less than half a mile from the spot where *Dark Sable* was moored.

Andreas set the first line so it was anchored at each side of the channel by a shackle and floated loosely across the water's surface directly in the path of any boat that would come by. Julia repeated the process farther down the channel. Soon all four lines had been set and floated lazily on the surface with the kelp so they were almost invisible.

"The nasty thing about polypro'," Andreas said, "is that when it wraps around a propeller, it usually fuses together so it's near impossible to cut with a knife." He smiled at Julia.

Back at the *King Fisher,* it was a long day. Julia lay on her bunk reading, keeping one ear open for the sound of a motor. That night she and her dad turned in early. Andreas slept in the wheelhouse with his rifle in the corner, the radio tuned to channel 51.

Jim brought the inflatable alongside the Fisheries boat and cut the motor. "Gillnetter" looked much bigger up close. On the side of her wheelhouse was her real name, *Juan Perez.* An officer in a dark blue uniform took the bow line from George.

"Pretty nice boat handling," the officer said, as Jim climbed aboard. "You must be the fellow who had all the adventures yesterday."

Jim glanced sideways at George.

"News spreads fast," said George, and introduced Jim to Officer Sharp. Then he asked, "Where's Tex now?"

"He's gone on with the skipper to coordinate things with the Coast Guard and pick up the night vision scope you requested. The skipper likes your plan."

Jim followed George below deck. The Fisheries boat was neater than *King Fisher,* but not nearly as comfortable. It reeked of oil and polish, and everything not in use had been put away in its place. The cabin wall was lined with old photographs of the *Juan Perez* with her former uniformed crews sitting in neat rows looking straight at the camera. Jim perched on the edge of a vinyl seat and sipped from a warm mug of hot chocolate placed before him by a friendly looking cook. He was listening to George discuss plans with Officer Sharp when Barry West walked into the cabin and slapped him on the shoulder.

"Quite the hero, huh?" Barry grinned.

Jim was pleased to see Barry and to learn that the

plan was that Barry, George, and Jim would leave Rose Harbour and go to Anthony Island—an ancient Haida village that was now a World Heritage Site near the west side of the entrance to Louscoone Inlet. There, they would set up an observation post.

Once they were in place, they could radio back to the Coast Guard cutter and the Fisheries protection boat, which would remain at Rose Harbour until dark, then sneak in behind the Gordon Islands on the eastern side of the mouth of Louscoone. There the two boats were to remain hidden until the watchers on Anthony Island sprang the trap. And if needed, Jim and George would set Tex's contingency plan in motion.

At noon a helicopter arrived from the mainland with two Royal Canadian Mounted Police (RCMP) officers from Prince Rupert. George picked them up from the beach and Jim watched the new arrivals settle awkwardly on the pontoons of the inflatable.

They were both heavy-looking men. One had a little clipped mustache, and the other was so clean-shaven his face was pink. Once on board, the officers walked past Jim without noticing him. They put their yellow-banded hats side by side on the table in the galley, then sat down and pulled piles of papers from fat briefcases.

"So where are the witnesses?" the RCMP officer with the mustache asked loudly.

"This is Jim," said George.

"And how old is Jim?" asked the officer.

"I am twelve," Jim responded.

The officer did not appear to notice that Jim had spoken.

"This is the only witness?" the officer asked George.

"No," said Jim. "Julia was there too, but she's back aboard *King Fisher*."

"Julia. Who's Julia?" he said, still addressing George.

"Julia is not here. She's ten years old," George said.

"Ten?" The officer's pen stopped in the middle of a word.

"That's right."

"Did any adult, uhh"—the officer seemed to be searching for the right word—"take the time to verify what these children saw?"

"No," said George frostily. "They are reliable kids and there hasn't been time anyway."

"I see. But this means you have called together the RCMP, the Department of Fisheries, and the Coast Guard for an operation that has already cost thousands of taxpayers' dollars, based on the unconfirmed report of two children?"

George's face bore a grim expression. "It was not my idea to invite the RCMP," he snapped. "I'm sure if you would rather be issuing parking tickets in Prince Rupert, Fisheries can handle it."

The officer put down his pen and glared at George. "Let's hear the evidence to date," he said, motioning to Jim.

Both officers made notes and took turns asking Jim questions. When they heard about his turning on the gas taps, the well-scrubbed officer turned red.

"Don't you think that was wrong? That gasoline was not yours."

"They were poachers," said Jim.

"We don't know that yet."

"They had undersized abalone in their freezer."

"So you say."

Jim looked to George for help.

"I might remind you," said George, "this is a friendly witness—not a suspect. What's more, he does know what an undersized abalone looks like."

"Tell us what happened after you opened the tap," said the officer with the mustache, ignoring George's intrusion.

When they heard that the man with the tattoos had a gun, their interest picked up. "What sort of gun?"

"I don't know—I guess it was a hunting rifle. It had one of those telescopic sights."

"This sounds like something for the ERT," said the pink-faced officer.

"What is the ERT?" asked Jim.

"Emergency Response Team," he replied.

"Maybe we should bring in the Navy and Air Force as well," said George.

"No need to be sarcastic."

At that moment, three men entered the cabin. Jim guessed that one was Captain Arnold of the Department of Fisheries. George, he knew, had a deep respect for him. The two men shook hands warmly and George introduced Jim.

"Congratulations," the captain said. "You and your young friend seem to have made quite a breakthrough."

The other two men were Coast Guard: one a burly bearded officer, the other a young lieutenant. They nodded curtly to the RCMP officers.

"Seems we're only missing a delegation from the Parks Department," said the burly man, who Jim figured was the captain of the Coast Guard cutter.

George rolled his eyes and caught Barry by the sleeve, trying to stifle a laugh.

"We've got to get going," George said. "It's four o'clock and a full hour to Anthony Island." And he walked out.

"Excuse me," Jim said, slipping unnoticed from the table and joining George outside.

"You're not going anywhere without me," he said anxiously.

George laughed. "Don't worry, I wouldn't leave you with those jerks."

"Just checking."

A big red and yellow Coast Guard vessel lay alongside. Tex was leaning over the rail of the Fisheries boat, smoking a cigarette.

"I didn't know you smoked those horrible things," said Jim.

"Don't usually," he said. "Just when I'm around too many bureaucrats."

Tex looked critically at the mass of polypropylene rope coiled in the bottom of the inflatable. "It's a bit heavy," he said. "But then, if she's a big one, that will be all the better."

Barry tossed a plump duffel bag into the bow of the inflatable and stepped aboard.

"And remember, if you need some extra light, just give a yell," said Tex. "I got lots of fireworks."

"I thought you didn't fly around here at night," said George.

"For you guys, I'd do anything. Just press my button."

"On channel 51, okay?"

"Fifty-one," Tex confirmed.

George passed down a bulky case and tripod, and then lowered himself into the inflatable. Jim started the motor, and Tex tossed in the bow line. Jim could feel the inflatable working against extra weight as he urged it up to planing.

"You're pretty good with this thing," Barry observed. "I guess it helps when you spend all your life with boats, eh?"

George tossed Jim a sly wink.

They headed west and then south down the broad channel. The inflatable skimmed the wave tops, motors whining smoothly. As the channel widened and the broad Pacific Ocean came into view, a breeze picked up and huge swells slid beneath them like gently undulating hills. They passed a flat rocky island where a navigation light flashed from a tower. Breakers exploded on its jagged foreshore and tugged the kelp into patterns like a chorus of sea snakes. Gulls rose from their nests, and a squadron of black cormorants flopped off their perches and circled defiantly.

Down the steep coast of Kunghit Island to the south, white foam licked the rocks and a pale haze softened the distant, wind-sculpted forest.

As they set a course for Anthony Island, a procession of gigantic swells swept in from some distant storm. Jim had never felt ocean swells before and shot an anxious glance at George, who sat with his chin in the air, sniffing the fresh ocean breezes like a hungry hound at a kitchen window.

George looked at Jim and grinned. "You're right. It *is* great," he said.

sixteen

SKUNG GWAII

They were crossing the huge waves at over twenty knots. At the bottom of the troughs, Jim could see nothing but walls of dark water towering over them. But from the crests, the view extended from Louscoone Inlet and down almost to Cape St. James at the end of the Queen Charlottes. Ahead, dark, forested Anthony Island grew closer, and more mysterious by the minute.

The waves diminished as the inflatable reached shelter at the eastern tip of the island. George took the wheel for the last hundred yards, and guided the boat toward a mass of rocks and two headlands occupied by gnarled trees. A quiet cove with a sweeping gravel beach opened up before them.

Jim's eyes opened wide. Above the beach he could see huge silvery totem poles as tall as trees leaning at crazy angles, half consumed by encroaching vegetation, but still seeming to guard what was left of the old Haida village of Ninstints. Jim felt the hair on the back of his neck start to prickle.

George throttled back and turned abruptly to the right, behind some rocks into a narrow channel leading to a steep ramp of round boulders, squeezed between two shoulders of rock. Barry leapt out and dragged the bow up the beach while George tilted the motors so the propellers wouldn't touch on the rocks.

At the top of the beach lay a huge pile of dark tubular bull kelp. George and Barry dragged armloads of it down and laid it across the ramp. George then set up a block and tackle, securing one end to an eye in the fiberglass bottom of the inflatable and the other to a sturdy tree. How easily the heavy boat slid up the bed of kelp! At the top of the beach, George had arranged several weathered logs so they formed parallel rollers across supporting rails of driftwood. With just one adjustment of the block and tackle, they hauled the inflatable over the rolling logs and up into the trees. They then dragged it around so it faced down the slope on its rollers, ready to be launched at a moment's notice. To finish, George cut some bushes and laid them in front of the boat so its red shape could not be seen from the water.

While George and Barry unloaded their gear, Jim wandered off to explore the nearby forest. He hadn't gone far into the trees when suddenly he froze. A tall Indian man dressed in blue jeans and a black T-shirt stood watching him from the shadows, a faint smile on his face.

"Wh-who are you?" stammered Jim.

"Who are you?" the man retorted, his voice soft and deep.

"I'm Jim Martin. I work with Fisheries."

The man laughed and walked slowly to where George and Barry were sorting gear into three piles.

"So Fisheries is hiring boys now," he said, chuckling. "Hey there, George!"

George looked up and smiled.

"Winston!" he cried, striding over and pumping the man's hand vigorously. "They told me you were doing time here. Even got some mail for you somewhere."

He introduced Barry and Jim.

"Jim, Winston Michaels is the Haida Gwaii watchman. He's custodian of the island."

"We've met," said Winston, extending his hand to Jim.

The man's handshake was leathery and warm, and the dark skin around his eyes wrinkled with laugh lines. He wore his shiny black hair pulled back in a long ponytail.

"Welcome to Skung Gwaii," he said.

Jim looked puzzled.

"To where?"

"Skung Gwaii is the Haida name for this island," he said earnestly. "Haida Gwaii is our ancient name for the Queen Charlottes."

Then, turning to George, Winston asked, "So what are you up to this time? And how come you're sneaking around like this? You make a man nervous." He smiled to show he was only half serious. "You coming over for coffee?"

"Thanks. We've got to set up this scope at a high point first," said George. "Spotting for poachers. We need to be able to see all around. Where's the best place?"

Winston thought for a moment. "You want to see out to sea as well?"

"Definitely."

Winston nodded, then picked up the instrument case and tripod and set off through the forest. The others followed, loaded with the rest of the gear.

Jim wore his day pack with his sleeping bag tied beneath it, and in each hand he carried a plastic bag of food. Green moss carpeting the forest floor was so springy it reminded Jim of walking across his parents' bed when he was very young. A muted light filtered through the forest canopy and glowed on the moss tips. Jim had never seen so much moss. It seemed to cover everything except the leaves themselves.

Soon their small group picked up a leafy path which led past a recently built Haida longhouse that smelled of wood smoke. Jim stopped and stared at the huge logs. "Is that where you live?" Jim asked.

When Winston nodded, Jim said, "You sure build 'em strong!"

Swinging from a bough was a reclining chair with a splendid view of the offshore rocks and islands. They continued past the longhouse and reentered the woods.

After a short walk, they came upon the totem poles Jim had seen from the boat. They were standing in the open forest at the head of the quiet bay. Gray and half rotted, their paint had worn off long ago. Some of the poles sprouted vegetation from their deeply carved surfaces. When Jim had been in fourth grade, he'd had to reenact the raising of a totem pole for parents' night, using a cardboard model. Not until he stood beside a real pole did he realize what an enormous task that must have been. The poles were as wide as a door and as tall as a house.

"That one's a bear," said Winston, pointing. "And that's a raven. See the beak? It's kind of rotting away now."

Winston showed them smooth hollows in the forest floor and a clearing of deer-nibbled grass which marked the sites of old Haida lodges. "There used to be a prosperous village with over four hundred people here," said Winston. "That was before the white man came with all his diseases."

"Look at this," said George, drawing Jim to one side. He pointed to the base of a huge old tree blown over in a storm. Jim stared at the bleached roots with rocks held fast by brittle fingers of wood. His jaw dropped suddenly when he realized he was staring at the bleached bones of a human skeleton, curled up with knees against chin.

"Probably a slave," said Winston. "This island's full of old bones. And ghosts," he added darkly, casting a glance at Jim, who was still staring at the chalky remains.

The path faded to a hint of a trail as it climbed a hill on the southern part of the island. On the windward side facing the ocean, the trees were stunted by the wind and formed a dense mat above their heads. As they climbed to the summit, gaps appeared in the vegetation, offering a clear view up Louscoone Inlet and eastward to the light on Flatrock Island.

By climbing into the low branches of a stunted ancient hemlock that grew close to the summit, they could get a fine view of the sea both to the west and south. Near the big tree, George found a narrow ledge just wide enough for three sleeping bags. They suspended a jungle green tarp between four trees to protect the sleeping bags and spread another tarp on the ground to put their bags on.

Out of the gear bags, George pulled a marine VHF

radio and connected it to a battery. He tuned in to a scratchy weather forecast.

"They're talking about a southeaster coming through tonight," said George, looking up at the sky.

"Tomorrow," said Winston.

Barry opened the instrument case and removed a powerful night vision scope, which he carefully screwed onto the tripod. Two pairs of binoculars remained in the box.

"You boys sure have fancy toys," Winston said, shaking his head.

George switched to channel 51 on the big marine radio, and broke open a new packet of batteries, slipping six into the walkie-talkie on his belt. Then he reached into the bag and retrieved a package and some letters held with a rubber band and handed them to Winston, who glanced at the return addresses and stuffed the letters in his pocket to read later.

"Bannock!" he said, sniffing the package. "You know what bannock is?" he asked Jim.

Jim shook his head.

"It's Native bread. Makes you grow strong," he said.

Winston turned to George. "What is today anyway?"

George looked at his watch. "July 25," he said.

"Today is July 25?" Jim asked. He had turned pale.

"Yeah. Hey, what's up, Jim?" said George.

"Oh, it's just that July 24 was the day of the accident," said Jim.

Suddenly, desperate to be alone, Jim said, "May I go down to the beach?"

"Sure," said George, "but be back before dark."

seventeen

THE LOOKOUT

Jim bolted down the trail. He ran so fast down the steep trail that in places he felt like he was falling, yet somehow his legs kept him up. Soon he was pounding through the trees to the grassy clearing, and there he slowed to a walk. His throat burned as he sucked in breath. His cheeks were wet with tears. He could not believe he had forgotten. He stood still for a moment, eyes closed, and tried to picture his father's face. Nothing came. His mind was blank. He took a trail that went west to the water's edge.

In a daze, Jim walked out onto a rocky point. Terraces of surf swept over scattered rocky islets and dashed themselves at his feet. He stared down into the turmoil of water, kelp, and mussel-covered rocks. He thought of his father's prickly tweed coat, and those strong broad hands on the steering wheel. He'd looked just like he was sleeping except for the blood. Why couldn't he remember his father's face? How could he forget that, of all things? No, it wasn't that he had forgotten; he could not remember—that was different.

He wondered what else he had lost. He'd hardly thought of his mother or sister for days, or was it weeks? But they were still alive and at least he could remember how they looked. For months after the funeral, Jim had refused to believe his father had really died. He kept expecting him to come home in the evening. From denial, he learned sorrow, but it was safer to forget. And forgetting was almost complete. He felt so guilty, and so empty.

He sat on a ledge, and the tormented ocean seemed to draw him in. He thought of falling forward, of throwing himself into that cauldron below. A heaviness welled up from inside and his eyes felt full to bursting. From deep inside came a moan he hardly recognized. He put his head down on his arms and sorrow swept over him like a wave. For the first time since his father had died, he really cried. He cried for a long time.

And like all waves, the crying passed. He found himself remembering his father, pitching a fastball and then standing, hands on hips, with a look of total disbelief on his face as Jim whacked the ball and his dad watched the ball's flight to the edge of the ballpark.

Jim looked up. The sun was lost in a bank of gray cloud somewhere near the horizon. He stood and took several deep breaths. Waves rolled over the offshore rocks as they had done since long before his father or the owner of those bones beneath the uprooted tree was born. He glimpsed himself, a tiny point on an infinite time line. The fresh breeze invigorated him and the waves seemed to have cleared his mind.

He made his way back to the beach and, with a fierce energy, gathered rocks, making trips back to the end of the rocky point to pile them into a cairn. Soon he had built a tower that reached his shoulders. He placed the last pointed rock on the top, and stood back. A white tern lifted into the breeze and hovered above him.

"You'd love it here, Pop," he said aloud. Then he turned and walked back into the forest.

Jim climbed to the lookout and found Barry perched in the hemlock. He had the tripod legs lashed firmly to the branches and his eye pressed into the scope. Jim climbed up beside him.

"Can I have a look?" he asked.

Barry scooted along the branch to make room.

"She's out there, all right," he said. "Almost due west."

Jim put his eye to the scope. Lurking on the horizon was the dirty white superstructure of a ship.

"So this thing works at night too?" Jim asked.

"Yep. It magnifies the available light so everything looks like bright moonlight."

Jim pushed his eye to it again. "It's a big one," he said.

"Yes. And she's coming closer."

Jim climbed down again and removed a pair of binoculars from its case. He sat on his sleeping bag facing north and, propping his elbows on his knees, trained the glasses on the long arm of Louscoone Inlet. The inlet showed no sign of life, though a bend prevented him from seeing as far as the poachers' cabin.

George returned from having coffee with Winston.

He was relieved to see Jim and laid his big hand on Jim's head lightly as a greeting.

"What do you see?" he asked.

"Nothing up the inlet, but the ship seems to be moving in closer," Jim responded. George swung into the hemlock above Jim and put his eye to the scope.

"Aha," he said. "What a nice prize. If we can seize her, it will make them think twice before they dabble in our pond again."

Barry climbed to the ground and rummaged briefly through their food bag, pulling out three cans of ravioli in tomato sauce. He emptied the contents into a pot which he put on a small camp stove. Jim hadn't realized how hungry he was until Barry handed him a steaming bowl of pasta minutes later.

"Voila," he said. "In zee finest Italian tradisheeon!"

Jim took a bowl up to George, balancing two in one hand as he climbed the tree. "May I come with you in the boat tonight?" he asked, while they ate.

"I was afraid you were going to ask that," said George.

"Well, I can't really stay here on the radio. That's Barry's job. And I am your boatman, right?"

"Yeah, right," George responded uncomfortably.

"So what's the problem?"

"Same as before. It will be dangerous out there."

"You plan to steer the boat and handle the rope too?" Jim asked.

George shook his head.

"Then it's settled." He held out his hand. Reluctantly, George shook it.

Jim looked through the scope. The ship was noticeably closer now, and the setting sun broke through a gap in the approaching clouds and glowed fiery pink on some windows.

"Maybe you should try to get some sleep, Jim. I'll wake you when the action starts."

Jim took the empty bowls, wiped them with a clump of moss, then climbed down to where Barry crouched over the radio. He had the walkie-talkie standing by on channel 51 and scribbled notes on a pad as he listened to the big radio through headphones. As Jim approached, he raised his index finger to his lips.

Jim rolled out his sleeping bag, took off his dirty sneakers, put on some dry socks, and crawled into his bag, not the least convinced he would be able to doze off with so much action pending. But in seconds he was asleep, only half hearing Barry's excited voice as he relayed the message he had intercepted: Rendezvous between poachers and the ship confirmed. Location: two miles south of Anthony Island. Time: zero one hundred hours.

eighteen

THE CHASE

Come on, buddy. It's starting to happen."

The voice was George's. Jim opened his eyes wide and scrambled from his sleeping bag.

"What's happening?" he mumbled, feeling for his sneakers.

"The ship's in close and we've just intercepted a message saying the poachers' speedboat is leaving with the first of three loads of abalone."

Jim shivered and pulled on his jacket. "What's the time?" he asked.

"One o'clock."

Jim groped his way up the tree and perched next to Barry, whose eye was glued to the night vision scope. Barry moved aside to let Jim look. The bright ghostly vision of the ship rolling and almost disappearing behind the waves filled the scope. Men stood on the bridge, while others worked on deck.

"This thing is amazing," said Jim, staring into the darkness. Without the scope he thought he could just see the dark shape of the vessel, though she showed no lights.

"How far away is she?" he asked, peering into the darkness.

"About two miles," Barry guessed.

"Here comes the speedboat," called George. "Sounds like she is really heavily loaded."

Jim listened and could just make out the labored growl of an engine in the darkness off Louscoone. Barry disconnected the scope's eyepiece and coupled a camera in its place. Then he put his eye to the viewfinder and grunted with satisfaction.

"You mean you can take a photograph through that thing?"

"If you use super-fast film. It won't win any prizes, but it will be clear enough for the judge," he said, settling down to wait.

George joined them on the branch.

"They should be at the ship about now," he said. Barry put his eye to the camera.

"Yep, I can see them just coming alongside. It looks rough out there. Man, they look small beside that ship."

"Why don't we get going and arrest them now? Why wait for the second run?" Jim asked.

"We want to give them time to load the abalone into the ship's freezer," said George. "That way they're less likely to throw the evidence over the side before we board."

Clunk, whirr, went the camera. *Clunk, whirr. Clunk, whirr.*

George held the binoculars to his eyes. They were not as good as the night scope, but were an improvement on bare eyes.

"They've lowered a net and the men in the speedboat are loading the abs across," Barry reported. "They're leaving now. Boy, they sure don't hang around."

Jim strained to make out the angry snarl of a motor as the speedboat raced back up Louscoone Inlet for the second load. This time the pitch of the engine was higher—*wow, wow, wow*—as she ran unloaded into the troughs of waves.

"It's good that they are short of fuel," said Barry. "You should have heard them arguing about Fujita coming in this close. He wanted the speedboat to take the abalone out ten miles. The poachers insisted they didn't have enough gas and wanted him to go right up Louscoone."

"Okay, let's go," said George. "And remember, Barry, let us know as soon as they come alongside the ship."

Before they left, they set up the big radio in a box wedged between two branches near the night scope. George slipped the walkie-talkie into a waterproof bag and clamped it closed. Using only a very weak light, he and Jim groped their way down the hill to the trail, past the shadowy totems and Winston's darkened longhouse with its lingering smell of wood smoke. The night was dark, with no moon, and the stars were obscured by high clouds from the approaching weather system. They reached the inflatable and tossed aside the branches

"You pull the bow line," said George, putting his shoulder behind the transom.

"Figure you'll need a hand with that boat," said a voice from the darkness.

"Winston!" said George, with delight.

Winston took a handle near the stern of the inflatable and they slid it down the rollers, then he waded out and held the boat while Jim and George put on their floater suits.

During the afternoon, George had carefully coiled the polypropylene rope in the bottom of the boat, attaching a parachute-style sea anchor to one end.

George started the engines and Winston gave the boat a gentle push toward the narrow passage between the rocks. George and Jim each took an oar to fend off rocks and push the inflatable out into the bay. Then they slowly motored into the midst of a bed of bull kelp, where George cut the motors.

Held fast in the undulating mat of slippery tubes, the inflatable rocked gently. They stared into the blackness and waited, as the first fitful gusts of the sou'easter buffeted their faces.

"Okay, let's go over the plan," said George. "With luck they're going to give up when they see the Coast Guard and we won't be needed. If they run, though, we'll go after them. It will be your job to take us about one hundred yards upwind of the ship, then we make a pass across her bow and toss out the rope. You turn when I say, and not before. Is that clear?"

"Are we going to make the RCMP and Coast Guard guys mad at us?"

"Not if it works and nobody gets hurt."

Jim was beginning to have second thoughts. The darkness crept inside his skin and settled in his bones. Anthony Island hovered like a brooding dark creature that grew from a black sea. Again Jim's mind returned to the skeleton under the tree and goose bumps prickled his arms.

"The tourists are going to visit mother," crackled Barry's voice on the walkie-talkie.

"Here they come," said George. "Listen."

Faintly Jim could hear the *warr, warr, warr* of the loaded speedboat going through big waves.

Jim sat with his hand on the starter button, listening as the motorboat growled past them. There followed an unbearable wait, interrupted by a message from Barry:

"The tourists are with mother. Gillnetter, seiner! Go for it!"

On the other side of the Gordon Islands, the motors of the darkened Fisheries and Coast Guard cutters hit full power as they broke cover for the rendezvous. An age passed without a sound reaching George and Jim in the inflatable. Finally Jim's sharp ears picked up the throb of the cutter's big diesels.

"Okay," George said calmly. "Let's go."

Jim pushed the starter button. The propellers chopped a swath of phosphorescence as they disturbed millions of tiny plankton.

"Mother is running," crackled the radio. "The tourists are escaping."

"Hit it," George snapped.

Jim jammed the throttle forward and the inflatable sprang like a racehorse at the starting gate.

"Keep left a bit. There are rocks off there."

Jim peered ahead into the darkness. He didn't like racing into waves he could not see. A few minutes, and the inflatable was clear of the rocks off Anthony Island. Suddenly a searchlight from the Coast Guard cutter pierced the night with a brilliant blue-white beam, illuminating the Korean ship as she was making a tight turn a mile ahead of the inflatable. A second light, this one from the Fisheries vessel, cut across the water and settled on the speedboat as it sped up Louscoone Inlet, its occupants heaving bags of frozen abalone over the side as they went.

Jim headed straight for the trawler, now clearly lit and charging seaward amid bursts of spray. The Coast Guard cutter lay off to their left, lagging a mile behind the trawler and losing ground. Jim gripped the wheel, his heart pounding as their quarry appeared and disappeared behind the waves. He glanced at George, who slapped him gently on the back and then picked up the radio.

"Tex, this is George. We sure could use some extra light out here."

"You betcha!" crackled the pilot's voice.

Barry, perched in the old hemlock atop Anthony Island, could see the Coast Guard cutter was losing ground to the trawler. Unless the inflatable could stop her, she would be almost out of sight of land by dawn. Through the scope, he could see the inflatable moving up fast. Big swells, moving in ahead of the cold front, were causing huge walls of spray to fly off the bow of the trawler, slowing her down each time she plunged.

He settled back to watch the chase. Within minutes the inflatable was running next to the trawler, a mouse beside an elephant. Barry snapped photographs: *Clunk, whirr. Clunk, whirr.*

Jim gripped the wheel and watched the trawler's gigantic rusty hull pitch and lunge against the waves.

The light from the Coast Guard cutter cast harsh shadows but was growing weaker as it grew more distant.

"Cut in behind!" yelled George.

Jim swung the wheel and they skidded across the top of a huge swell into the flattened turbulence of the ship's wake. Jim's heart leapt as Tex's helicopter thundered overhead with a sudden roar. The ocean exploded with vivid white light as a flare hung in the sky.

Like an overexposed black-and-white movie in slow motion, the trawler's name appeared on her stern: *Toku Maru,* Seoul, South Korea.

"Port! More to port!" yelled George.

Jim looked over his shoulder. They were too close. He could feel the pounding motors of the ship through the deck of the inflatable. He could see men staring from the ship's bridge, which towered like an apartment building above them. Fear gripped Jim, and for a moment he froze. The throbbing monster sucked them in.

"You're too close. Keep out farther!" roared George. Jim snapped to and veered away. He started talking to himself: Don't look directly at the trawler, or next time you won't be able to turn away. They moved up the port side of the ship, past the bridge, and out beyond the lunging bow.

"That's it. Hold her steady . . . hold her steady. Now! Hard to starboard!"

George had moved aft and now stood astride the coil of floating rope. Just when Jim turned the wheel, George flung the sea anchor into the ocean. With a buzz the rope wriggled into the sea like an angry blue serpent.

Jim shot a glance to his right: the bow of the trawler was heading straight for them, luridly lit by two more flares that had been shot from the helicopter.

"She's turning!" he screamed, as the ship yawed hard to starboard and continued to head straight for them. The last of the rope flicked over the side and the inflatable jumped ahead, lightened of her load. They were beyond the turning arc of the *Toku Maru* now, and turned to run down the starboard side of the ship.

"Slow down," yelled George.

Jim throttled back and watched as the ship hauled on by and headed for the open sea. "It missed!" he cried. "She turned and we missed."

George stood high and searched the foam for the blue rope.

"There it is. Quick! Let's try again!" he cried.

They found the end of the blue rope and George fished it out of the sea and began hauling in furiously, piling the line in the middle of the inflatable so it would spill out without tangling.

To the east, the Coast Guard cutter was still more than a mile distant. Jim was vaguely aware of the walkie-talkie crackling away furiously as those aboard tried to figure out what George and Jim were doing.

Finally the sea anchor flooded aboard.

"I'm done!" called George. "Get in front of them again!"

Jim jammed the throttle forward and they set off in pursuit of the *Toku Maru,* now almost a half mile to seaward. George grabbed the walkie-talkie.

"Give us some light in front of her, Tex," he cried.

"Roger!"

"You've got to take her in closer, Jim. Otherwise she'll turn again."

Jim knew what to do this time. As they came along the port side of the huge trawler, he watched her from the corner of his eye. The swells seemed even larger than before, and the wind was freshening from the south. The throb of the ship's diesels seemed to pulse through his veins.

A flare. Brilliant light caught the edges of the mountainous seas. Spray was being tossed aside from the *Toku Maru* like gigantic lace curtains. He stole a glance over his shoulder. George was in position astride the coil of rope, sea anchor in his hand. Just a few boat-lengths away, the ocean seethed white alongside the fast-moving trawler.

Jim planned to start his run from slightly behind the bow this time, so even if she turned to port, they would get her. As they drew level with the bow, a huge wave exploded, drenching them in a wall of spray. Jim squinted and began his turn, aiming for a point barely twenty feet ahead of the bow as it reared clear of the water in the the bright light.

He sensed George tossing the sea anchor, felt the drag on their speed, and adjusted his course. They were dead ahead of the *Toku Maru* now and rising fast up a watery cliff. Jim risked a look and found himself staring down onto the cluttered foredeck of the ship. She was really close. He swung the wheel, but the drag of the line spinning over the side slowed the inflatable.

In slow motion he saw the ship's bow erupt through the wave like a bomb, then they were falling, dropping down the other side, through a wall of settling spray, with their engines screaming. They were clear. The last of the rope jerked from the boat and they were in the still air on the lee of the ship, with the fumes from the galley and the throb of her engine.

"We got her this time for sure," Jim cried hopefully.

"It still has to wrap around the propeller," George cautioned, moving up next to Jim. They watched her pass.

All of a sudden, the *Toku Maru*'s engine took on a new pitch. The big ship sagged in the stern, then wallowed, and began to roll wildly.

"We got her! We got her!" Jim hollered.

George gave a whoop, and picked up the radio. "We caught the trawler. She's dead in the water!" he announced triumphantly.

The Coast Guard cutter soon arrived and took up a position to seaward of the *Toku Maru*. A line was tossed to crewmen on the bow of the stricken ship which was beginning to drift toward the rocky coast of Anthony Island. Using the lifeline, the crew then hauled a sturdy towing cable across.

Meanwhile, Jim and George motored back to Anthony Island, just as a strip of clear sky above the mountains turned orange and the southeasterly wind started to pick the tops off the waves.

Jim's hands shook on the wheel and his heart fluttered wildly in his chest. As they entered the cove at Anthony Island, he yelled at the top of his lungs, "Yahoo!"

George was smiling broadly as they beached in front of the totem poles. The gray light of dawn revealed Winston standing at the edge of the beach. The first drops of rain spiked the water. "That looked like a pretty exciting ride you had out there," he said, hauling the bow of the inflatable up onto the gravel.

"You watched through the night glasses?" asked Jim.

"Who needs night glasses? You fellas lit up the whole coast!"

Barry appeared out of the darkness, carrying the radio and night vision scope under his arm.

"Congratulations!" he said. "For a moment there, it looked like you had gone right under her."

"Felt like it too," Jim admitted.

Suddenly there was a squawk from the walkie-talkie. "This is oyster calling. The tourists are making a break for it." The voice was Julia's.

nineteen

SHOTS FROM THE FOREST

Several times during the night, Andreas had awakened and checked the glowing dial of his watch. He noticed the first uneasy puffs of the approaching storm and let out another fifty yards of anchor chain, then went back to his bunk.

A message from Barry brought him to his feet so fast his head spun. He listened intently to the hiss of the airwaves, then smiled as he heard Barry spring the trap. It was after two o'clock when he heard that the speedboat was breaking not for the mainland but back up Louscoone Inlet; it was time to put the next part of the plan into action.

"Time to wake up, Jewel," he said, giving Julia a gentle shake.

Collecting his hunting rifle and a packet of shells, Andreas switched off the lights and turned to climb into the skiff.

Julia flung her arms around her father's neck. "Be careful," she whispered.

Andreas put an arm around her shoulder and planted a kiss on her forehead. "They won't even know where I am," he said.

Andreas went over the side of *King Fisher* and arranged the oars, leaving Julia to return, grim faced, to the wheelhouse, where she stared out the window, radio microphone in hand. Her instructions were simple: stand by on the radio and send a message out as soon as she was sure the *Dark Sable* was making a break for open water.

Andreas was full of misgivings as he rowed away from *King Fisher*. He hated leaving Julia alone but could think of no better alternative. They knew that at least one of the poachers was armed, and by taking the initiative, Andreas reasoned he would have a better chance of controlling the situation and keeping the poachers away from *King Fisher*.

The skiff ground against barnacle-covered rocks on the darkened shore of Slim Inlet. Andreas stepped out into the shallows and dragged the little boat into the bushes.

Carefully, he picked his way up the shore. For half an hour he made good speed, though in places the rising tide forced him into the woods, where he made so much noise crashing through the salal he was sure they could hear him.

A stiff southerly breeze soon came down the inlet, while above the mountains on the mainland, a shrinking band of clear sky was turning yellow, then orange. He had just passed the first of the floating lines, barely visible in the early light of day, when he heard the *Dark Sable*'s motor start up.

No longer worrying about noise, he pushed into the salal and selected a vantage point well back from the water. Slowly and deliberately, he loaded five shells into his rifle and settled back against a big rotten log.

It wasn't long before the *Dark Sable* came into view, pushing a sizable wall of water before her. She churned over the first rope, passing with no apparent effect. Then on to the second. Nothing. Then the third. Andreas began to wonder if the trick would work: some fishing boats he knew were fitted with cages around their propellers to prevent fouling on loose lines.

Dark Sable motored on until suddenly, with a bang, one of the shackles banged into the hull and then started pounding against it. Next came a change in the engine sound. For a moment the engine revved under the load.

Andreas smiled. "That's right," he thought aloud. "Make her nice and tight."

The man with the tattoos burst out of the wheelhouse and leaned over the stern. A gust of wind funneled down the valley and turned the *Dark Sable* sideways in the channel. Andreas heard the man curse, yelling an order as a crew member ran forward. The anchor clattered over the side to prevent the boat from being blown onto the rocks. Raindrops speckled the gray waters of the inlet and patted the leaves around Andreas like an army of insects.

One of the crew appeared on deck zipping up a wet suit. In one hand he carried a mask and snorkel, in the other a knife. The wind gusted and *Dark Sable* swung on her anchor to face into the wind.

Stealthily, Andreas moved back into the woods, looking for a position that would both offer a clear view of the boat and keep him hidden. He found a recent windfall and made himself comfortable behind it. His heart pounded and his breath came in short gasps. With an effort he slowed his breathing, removed the protective caps from the scope, and peered through the cross hairs to where the man in the wet suit was climbing over the stern, knife in hand.

Aiming carefully at the water a few inches from the man's foot, Andreas squeezed the trigger. With a bang, the rifle bucked against his shoulder, and a spout of water lifted eight feet into the air.

Pandemonium broke out aboard *Dark Sable*. The man in the wet suit dove headfirst onto the deck, smacking his head against the raised hatch. The others threw themselves flat on their faces and wriggled to the protection of the boards along the scuppers. They had no idea where the shot had come from, so they didn't know where to hide.

"Who are you? What do you want?" the tattooed man finally yelled, raising his head slightly and peering into the forest.

Andreas said nothing, confident no one on board would risk moving without knowing exactly where the shots were coming from or how many people were out there.

"Damn it, man! What do you want?"

Silence.

Fifteen minutes passed. Faintly, the flutter of a helicopter motor reached Andreas's ears. Soon, with a deafening roar, the RCMP chopper thundered over the trees and hovered directly above *Dark Sable*. A rope ladder unrolled and two RCMP officers scrambled down and onto the deck to make the arrests. Andreas slipped away quietly, retracing his steps to the skiff.

twenty

TEX DROPS IN FOR BREAKFAST

Five men were captured aboard the *Dark Sable* and another twenty arrested on the *Toku Maru.* Both vessels were subsequently confiscated. Newspaper reporters flew in and interviewed everyone involved in the capture, especially Jim and Julia.

Four days after the arrests, when most of the fuss had died down, George, Jim, Julia, and Andreas sat together once again at the breakfast table of *King Fisher,* discussing the capture of the "Abalone Gang," as the poachers had come to be known.

The deep, now-familiar sound of Tex's Hughes 500 interrupted the meal, and everybody came up on deck and watched their friend touch down on the beach.

"Can't finish a meal in peace these days," Andreas muttered, smiling.

"I'll get him," Jim volunteered, jumping into the inflatable.

Climbing into the boat, Tex gripped a canvas sack. He sat on a sponson and took a long, deliberate look at Jim.

"Sure seems a long time ago that I brought a real green city kid in here in old Huey," he said.

"You must be thinking of someone else," Jim retorted.

In the galley, Tex tossed a bundle of letters on the table and poured himself a cup of coffee while everyone sorted through the mail. Jim had three letters from his mother and one from his sister.

"Oh, and I thought you might like to read some newspapers," Tex said casually.

There on the front page of the *Vancouver Sun* was a truly spectacular photo of the *Toku Maru* with the inflatable speeding across her wake—one of Barry's night scope shots.

"And look at this now," Tex said, tossing down a copy of *The Province.* The banner headline read: "BOY 12, GIRL 10, CAPTURE PIRATE FISHING BOAT."

"But we didn't do it all," Julia exclaimed with raised eyebrows.

"You must have. See, it's here in writing," Tex said, chuckling.

Jim read the story out loud. "But this isn't at all how it was," he said.

"Welcome to the world of popular journalism. What do they say? Never let the facts get in the way of a good story?" They all looked at one another for a moment, then burst out laughing.

Tex had more in his bag.

"Why don't you see if these fit," he said, tossing two plastic bags on the table.

Jim and Julia each opened a bag, and their faces lit up as two neatly folded brown flight suits tumbled onto the table. QUEEN CHARLOTTE ISLANDS AIR SERVICE was embroidered on the pocket, and there were lots of pockets and sleeves for pencils.

"It's perfect, it's perfect!" whooped Julia, giving Tex a big hug.

"Looks like it was made for me," said Jim, as he finished zipping himself in.

"I guess you could say that," Tex responded with a quick wink.

Jim's letters from his mother told of the daily happenings back home. While the others chatted, he sat lost in the details of a distant world.

"What's news?" asked George.

"Got three letters from my mom," said Jim.

"Me too," George smiled.

Jim laughed. "I guess that figures. Do yours say anything?"

"Of course they say something," said George. "Your mom warns me that you sometimes take reckless risks and to keep an eye on you."

They all laughed.

"And she says she's training to use computers."

"Yeah, that's good news," Jim agreed.

"Also, there's a letter from my old university professor offering me a job. He's recommended me for a contract to do reef research in the Turks and Caicos islands when this contract is finished."

"Turks and Caicos?"

"In the South Bahamas, north of the Caribbean."

"It's hot there, isn't it?"

"And the water is clear and warm."

"Are you gonna need a boatman there by any chance?"

"And crew. You're going to need a crew you can trust," Julia added.

"Well, I don't know. That would depend on what kind of grades you guys get this next year. Must say I would like to have the best crew and boatman in the business with me."

"Alright!" Jim and Julia yelled, together.

George looked at his watch. "Come to think of it, there's still a heap of abalone to be counted out there. We'd better get going."

ABOUT THE AUTHOR

John Dowd has received wide recognition as the author of *Sea Kayaking: A Manual for Long Distance Touring* (1981), the "bible" of the sport. Born and raised in New Zealand, Dowd traveled throughout the world for fifteen years, working as a freelance writer and photographer, a diver in the North Sea, a safari tour operator in South America, and an Outward Bound instructor.

In 1980, he established Ecomarine, North America's first ocean kayaking specialty shop, in Vancouver, British Columbia. In 1984, he cofounded *Sea Kayaker,* the sport's first magazine. His articles on sea kayaking have appeared in numerous publications, including *Wooden Boat* and *Nautical Quarterly.*

In 1990, Dowd turned his energies to writing books full time. His first book for young readers was *Ring of Tall Trees,* a suspenseful story that mixes Northwest Indian lore with a present-day struggle to save an ancient forest. He is currently working on a sequel to *Abalone Summer,* a thriller set in the Caribbean. He lives outside Vancouver in a log cabin on a mountainside with his wife, his two children, and two Great Pyrenees dogs.